CORNE[LL WOOLRICH]

His name represe[nts] chilling encounters on the dark and sultry landscape of urban America in the '30s and '40s. Author of more than 100 stories, novelettes, and books—many dramatized on such classic radio shows as *Climax* and *Suspense*, on TV's *Alfred Hitchcock Presents*, and in great films like *The Bride Wore Black*, *Rear Window*, and *Phantom Lady*—Woolrich is in a class by himself.

CORNELL WOOLRICH

"HIS WRITING GOES RIGHT THROUGH YOU LIKE A SHRIEK IN THE NIGHT. SOMETIMES YOU EVEN WISH YOU COULD FORGET IT, BUT YOU CAN'T."

Dorothy Salisbury Davis

CORNELL WOOLRICH

"HE CAN DISTILL MORE TERROR, MORE EXCITEMENT, MORE DOWNRIGHT NAIL-BITING SUSPENSE OUT OF EVEN THE MOST COMMONPLACE HAPPENINGS THAN NEARLY ALL HIS COLLEAGUES AND COMPETITORS."

Ellery Queen

CORNELL WOOLRICH

one of the truly great and truly original American writers . . . now coming back to readers everywhere from Ballantine Books.

Rear Window

And Four Short Novels

BALLANTINE BOOKS • NEW YORK

TABLE OF CONTENTS

INTRODUCTION
FRANCIS M. NEVINS, JR.

*N*_{oir}.

Any French dictionary will tell you that the word's primary meaning is black, dark, or gloomy. But since the mid-1940s and when used with the nouns *roman* (novel) or *film*, the adjective has developed a specialized meaning, referring to the kind of bleak, disillusioned study in the poetry of terror that flourished in American mystery fiction during the 1930s and 1940s and in American crime movies during the forties and fifties. The hallmarks of the *noir* style are fear, guilt, and loneliness, breakdown and despair, sexual obsession and social corruption, a sense that the world is controlled by malignant forces preying on us, a rejection of happy endings and a preference for resolutions heavy with doom but always redeemed by a breathtakingly vivid poetry of word (if the work was a novel or story) or image (if it was a movie).

During the 1940s, many American books of this sort were published in French translation in a long-running series called the *Série Noire*, and at the end of World War II, when French film enthusiasts were exposed for the first time to Hollywood's cinematic analogue of those books, they coined *film noir* as a phrase to describe the genre. What Americans of those years tended to dismiss as commercial entertainments the French saw as profound explorations of the heart of darkness, largely because *noir*, so intimately related to the themes of

French existentialist writers like Sartre and Camus, spoke to the despair that so many in Europe were experiencing after the nightmare years of war and occupation and genocide. By the early 1960s, cinephiles in the United States had virtually made an American phrase out of *film noir* and had acclaimed this type of movie as one of the most fascinating genres to emerge from Hollywood. *Noir* directors—not only the giants, like Alfred Hitchcock (in certain moods) and Fritz Lang, but relative unknowns, like Edgar G. Ulmer, Jacques Tourneur, Robert Siodmak, Joseph H. Lewis, and Anthony Mann —were hailed as visual poets whose cinematic style made the bleakness of their films not only palatable but fantastically exciting.

Several first-rate books on this movie genre have recently been published in the United States [the best is Foster Hirsch's *Dark Side of the Screen: Film Noir* (1981)], and one can attend courses on *film noir* at any number of colleges. But there has not yet developed a corresponding interest in the doom-haunted novels and tales of suspense in which *film noir* had its roots. Although Raymond Chandler, the poet of big-city corruption, and James M. Cain, the chronicler of sexual obsession, have received the fame they deserve, the names of countless other *noir* writers are known only to specialists.

Names like Cornell Woolrich.

Woolrich was born on December 4, 1903, to parents whose marriage collapsed in his youth. Much of his childhood was spent in Mexico with his father, a civil engineer. When he was eight, the experience of seeing a traveling French company perform Puccini's *Madame Butterfly* in Mexico City gave Woolrich a sudden sharp insight into color and drama and his first sense of tragedy. Three years later he understood fully that someday, like Cio-Cio-San, he too would have to die, and from then on he was haunted by a sense of doom that never left him.

During adolescence he lived with his mother and maternal relatives in New York City, and in 1921 he entered Columbia College, where he began writing fiction. He then quit school, in his junior year, to pursue his dream of becoming another F. Scott Fitzgerald. His first novel, *Cover Charge* (1926), chronicled the lives and loves of the Jazz Age's gilded youth in the manner of his and his whole generation's literary idol. This book was followed by the prizewinning *Children of the Ritz* (1927), whose success propelled Woolrich to Hollywood as a screenwriter, a job at which he failed, and into a brief marriage, at which he failed even worse. Before long, he fled back to New York and his mother. For the next quarter century he lived with her in residential hotels, going out only when it was absolutely essential, trapped in a bizarre love-hate relationship that dominated his external world just as the inner world of his later fiction reflects in its tortured patterns the strangler grip in which his mother and his own inability to love a woman held him.

From 1934 until his death, in 1968, this tormented recluse all but created what we know as *noir*, writing dozens of haunting tales of suspense, despair, and lost love, set in a universe controlled by diabolical powers. During the thirties his work appeared only in pulp magazines, like *Black Mask* and *Detective Fiction Weekly*. Then, beginning with *The Bride Wore Black* (1940), he launched his so-called Black Series of suspense novels—which appeared in France as part of the *Série Noire* and led the French to acclaim him as a master of bleak poetic vision. Much of his reputation still rests on those novels and on the other suspense classics originally published under his pseudonyms William Irish and George Hopley. Throughout the forties and fifties, Woolrich's publishers issued numerous hardcover and paperback collections of his short stories. Many of his novels and tales were

adapted into movies, including such fine *film noirs* as
Tourneur's *Leopard Man* (1943), Siodmak's *Phantom
Lady* (1944), Roy William Neill's *Black Angel* (1946),
Maxwell Shane's *Fear in the Night* (1947), and, most
famous of all, Hitchcock's *Rear Window* (1954). Even
more of Woolrich's work was turned into radio and later
into television drama. But despite overwhelming finan-
cial and critical success, his life remained a wretched
mess, and when his mother died, in 1957, he cracked.
From then until his own death, eleven years later, he
lived alone, his last year spent in a wheelchair after the
amputation of a gangrenous leg, wracked by diabetes
and alcoholism and homosexual self-contempt. But the
best of his final "tales of love and despair" are still gifted
with the magic touch that chills our hearts, and in a title
for a story he never wrote he captured the essence of his
world and the world of *noir* in six words:
"First you dream, then you die."

Woolrich wrote all sorts of stories, including quasi
police procedurals, rapid-action whizbangs, and tales of
the occult. But he is best known as the master of pure
suspense, the writer who could evoke with awesome
power the desperation of those who walk the city's darkened streets and the terror that lurks at noonday in the
most commonplace settings. In his hands, even such
clichéd storylines as the race to save the innocent person
from the electric chair and the amnesiac hunting his lost
self resonate with human anguish. Woolrich's world is a
feverish place where the prevailing emotions are loneliness and fear, and the prevailing action—as in his classics "Three O'Clock" (1938) and "Guillotine" (1939)—is
the race against time and death. His most characteristic
detective stories end with the realization that no rational
account of events is possible, and his suspense stories
tend to close with omnipresent terror.
The typical Woolrich settings are the seedy hotel, the

cheap dance hall, the run-down movie house, and the precinct station backroom. The dominant reality in his world is the Depression, and Woolrich has no peers when it comes to describing a frightened little guy in a tiny apartment with no money, no job, a hungry wife and children, and anxiety eating him like a cancer. If a Woolrich protagonist is in love, the beloved is likely to vanish in such a way that the protagonist not only can't find her but can't convince anyone she ever existed. Or, in another classic Woolrich situation, the protagonist comes to after a blackout—caused by amnesia, drugs, hypnosis, or whatever—and little by little becomes certain that he committed a murder or other crime while not himself. The police are rarely sympathetic; in fact, they are the earthly counterparts of the malignant powers above, and their main function is to torment the helpless.

All we can do about this nightmare we live in is to create, if we are very lucky, a few islands of love and trust to sustain us and help us forget. But love dies while the lovers go on living, and Woolrich excels at making us watch relationships corrode. He knew the horrors that both love and lovelessness can breed, yet he created very few irredeemably evil characters, for Woolrich identifies with whoever either loves or needs love, all of that person's dark side notwithstanding.

Purely as technical exercises, many of Woolrich's novels and stories are awful. They don't make the slightest bit of sense. And that, of course, is the point. Neither does life. Nevertheless, some of his tales, usually thanks to outlandish coincidence, manage to end quite happily. But since he never used a series character, the reader can never know in advance whether a particular Woolrich story will be light or dark, *allègre* or *noir*—which is one of many reasons why his stories are so hauntingly suspenseful.

Like the five collected here.

* * *

The connecting link between these tales is that many years after their first publication, all of them were filmed either by or under the auspices of the director of the finest suspense movies of all time—Alfred Hitchcock. Someone will eventually write a long article on the Hitchcock-Woolrich affinity. No doubt it will be full of suggestions about the common factors in their lives that drew both men to the *noir* view of the world: the harsh Catholic upbringing, with its instilled terror of death and the hereafter, and the longing for physical relationships that the obesity of the one and the homosexuality of the other seemed to put forever out of reach. This is not the place for such speculations. But it's clear that Hitchcock saw Woolrich as a prime source of filmable material, for between 1954 and 1958 he personally directed a full-length theatrical movie and a magnificent sixty-minute telefilm based on Woolrich tales, and his company adapted another three into half-hour filmed segments of the TV series *Alfred Hitchcock Presents*. It is these five Woolrich stories that are collected here.

"Rear Window" was the last written of the quintet but the first to come to Hitchcock's attention. It was first published in the February 1942 *Dime Detective* as "It Had to Be Murder." Two years later, Woolrich changed the title to the much more evocative "Rear Window" and included it in his early collection of short fiction, *After-Dinner Story* (1944), published under his William Irish pseudonym. Since then it's been reprinted regularly in other periodicals (*All Mystery*, for October–December 1950; *The Saint Detective Magazine*, for Winter 1953; and the February 1969 *Ellery Queen's Mystery Magazine*) and in anthologies, like Howard Haycraft and John Beecroft's monumental *Treasury of Great Mysteries* (1957). The story ranked high in a recent poll of the Mystery Writers of America organization to determine the favorite short crime tales of all time and was therefore reprinted again in the anthology based on this poll, *The Mystery Hall of Fame* (1983), edited by Bill Pronzini, Martin H. Greenberg, and Charles G. Waugh.

Much of this story's fame, of course, is due to Hitchcock's classic movie *Rear Window* (1954), starring James Stewart, as Jeffries; Grace Kelly, as his girl friend, Lisa; Thelma Ritter, as the friendly-snoopy visiting nurse, Stella; Wendell Corey, as Lieutenant Doyle; and Raymond Burr, as the murderer, Thorwald. Hitchcock and screenwriter John Michael Hayes expanded the Woolrich story into a two-hour film, by integrating into the movie's structure a host of major and minor characters and an abundance of themes that are absent from Woolrich's tale or at most hinted at. The Hitchcock device of limiting our viewpoint to what the immobilized Jeffries can see from the rear window of his apartment comes more or less directly from Woolrich. But Jeffries as Woolrich drew him is a man alone, with no one to talk to day in and day out except the kindly black houseman, Sam. By adding the Grace Kelly and Thelma Ritter characters and building up Wendell Corey's role as James Stewart's detective friend, Hitchcock opened the door to all the elements that set the movie apart.

Woolrich never tells us what Jeffries does for a living, but Hitchcock makes him a professional photographer, a man whose job involves a sort of spying on people, so it's completely in character for him to while away the long hot days and nights of his immobility by peering into his neighbors' lives through his telephoto lens. We, the viewers, are forced to see all that Jeffries sees and nothing else, and Hitchcock thereby tells us in effect that just as his likable protagonist is also a sick voyeur, so are all of us. There are hints of this motif in Woolrich's story. "Why is [Thorwald] so interested in other people's windows, I wondered detachedly. And of course an effective brake to dwelling on that thought too linger-

ingly clamped down almost at once: Look who's talking.
What about you yourself?" But Hitchcock transformed
the voyeurism theme into one of the central elements in
the film.

> JEFFRIES: I wonder if it's ethical to watch a man
> with binoculars and a long-focus lens. Do you sup-
> pose it's ethical even if you prove he *didn't* commit
> a crime?
> LISA: I'm not much on rear-window ethics.
> . . . Look at you and me, plunged into despair be-
> cause we find out a man *didn't* kill his wife. We're
> two . of the most frightening ghouls I've ever
> known.

Another central motif of the movie likewise stems
from the barest hint in the story. As presented by Woolrich, most of Jeffries's spying is concentrated on Thorwald, and the other neighbors into whose lives he peers
are given only a few poignant paragraphs. Hitchcock
creates more neighbors and makes each of them—Miss
Lonelyhearts, Miss Torso, the composer, the honey-
mooners, the middle-aged man and woman with the
dog—vivid characters in their own right. But the crucial
point is that each of these people or couples represents
Jeffries's vision of one of his own possible futures if he
makes a permanent commitment to Lisa. This motif,
which is fully elaborated in Donald Spoto's masterly *Art
of Alfred Hitchcock* (1976) and other critical works, has
no counterpart at all in Woolrich.

Rear Window is a first-rate movie in which Hitchcock
kept the basic Woolrich plot, the Did-He-or-Didn't-He
oscillations, and the hair-raising suspense climax but
grafted onto the structure all sorts of complex nuances
of theme and character and mood (the heat wave, the
steady stream of light, bantering dialogue with dark
implications) that turned the picture into something

quite different from the Woolrich version, which you are about to read.

"Change of Murder" was one of Woolrich's earliest crime stories, first published in *Detective Fiction Weekly* for January 25, 1936. It was included in *If I Should Die Before I Wake* (Avon Murder Mystery Monthly #31, 1945), a rare paperback collection published under the pseudonym William Irish, and in Frank Owen's mammoth anthology *Murder for the Millions* (1946). On May 21, 1950, during the infancy of television, a live TV adaptation was aired on *Video Theatre*, with a cast of unknowns headed by Bernard Nedell, Charles Jordan, and Alfred Hosson. As you'll see, the story's style and characters are much in debt to Damon Runyon, and its only touch of *noir* is the ironic ending, which Woolrich borrowed, not just this once but in several other stories too, from James M. Cain's 1934 classic, *The Postman Always Rings Twice*. But this kind of twist-in-the-tail yarn was precisely what the story editors of CBS-TV's *Alfred Hitchcock Presents* were looking for a few years later, and someone with a long memory recalled "Change of Murder." A thirty-minute film version, retitled "The Big Switch," was aired on the Hitchcock program January 8, 1956. Don Weis directed from a script by Richard Carr that radically altered the story line, and the lackluster cast was topped by George Mathews, George E. Stone, and Joseph Downing. Woolrich's story was reprinted once more, in *Mike Shayne Mystery Magazine* for January 1962, and now, after twenty-one years of oblivion, here it is again.

If I had to choose one short work of Woolrich for future generations to judge him by it would be "Three O'Clock," which for my money is the most powerful suspense story he (or anyone else) ever wrote. Paul Stapp is bound and gagged in his own basement, unable to move or even to scream, while the time bomb he himself set but is now unable to reach ticks closer and closer to three o'clock, when it will go off. And Woolrich makes us sit in that basement with him, counting the seconds until our own inevitable death. This unforgettable masterpiece of terror is one of the supreme classics of *noir* literature.

Its first appearance was in *Detective Fiction Weekly* for October 1, and Woolrich included it in his earliest collection of short stories, *I Wouldn't Be in Your Shoes* (1943), published under his William Irish by-line. A few years later it was reprinted in *The Avon Mystery Story Teller* (Avon pb #86, 1946) and in an anthology nominally edited by Boris Karloff, *And the Darkness Falls* (1946). At that point, the story was discovered by other media. On March 10, 1949, an excellent thirty-minute version starring Van Heflin was broadcast on CBS Radio's memorable series *Suspense*. Three weeks later, on March 31, a live TV adaptation with Steven Hill, Frances Reid, and Philip Bourneuf was seen (by the handful of people who had sets at that early date) on a dramatic series called *The Actors' Studio*. Late the same year, a matched pair of thirty-minute dramatizations was aired on ABC's joint radio-TV anthology *Presenting Boris Karloff*, also known as *Mystery Playhouse*, the radio version being heard November 30 and the TV production with the same cast being seen the following evening. Next came a sixty-minute live teledrama, broadcast June 18, 1951, on NBC-TV's *Robert Montgomery Presents*, starring Montgomery himself as Stapp and featuring Olive Deering and Vaughn Taylor. Montgomery had both directed and starred in some excellent *film noirs* of the forties, like *The Lady in the Lake* (1946) and *Ride the Pink Horse* (1947), and in 1948 he'd played the amnesiac protagonist in *Suspense*'s superb sixty-minute radio version of Woolrich's novel *The Black Curtain*. He would seem to have been a natural for the role of Stapp in "Three O'Clock." After all this exposure in the media it was predictable that publishers would recycle Woolrich's original story, which was reprinted in the short-lived mystery magazine *Verdict* (September 1953) and a few years later was included by Woolrich himself in another collection of his short fiction, *Nightmare* (1956).

It was apparently this book that brought the tale to Hitchcock's attention, and the following year he directed a sixty-minute film version that is not only the most faithful movie ever based on Woolrich but the most unremittingly suspenseful picture Hitchcock ever made. The film was retitled *Four O'Clock* for reasons unknown and broadcast September 30, 1957, on NBC-TV's dramatic series *Suspicion*. Francis Cockrell adapted the story for Hitchcock and E. G. Marshall starred, with Nancy Kelly and Richard Long in the principal supporting roles. In *Rear Window*, Hitchcock had expanded the Woolrich source story and altered its tone to suit his own needs, but this time Woolrich's tale perfectly captured the director's own existential terror before the specter of death, and the changes he made were minimal. Perhaps someday that film, pure Woolrich and pure Hitchcock at the same time, will be televised again as it deserves to be, but meanwhile, it's a pleasure to present once more the unforgettable story that Hitchcock adapted.

"He was possessed with a macabre humor," Woolrich's mystery-writing colleague Steve Fisher said of him, and for confirmation one need go no further than "Post-Mortem," which recounts the grisly search for a winning lottery ticket buried in a dead man's suit pocket. The story was first published in the April 1940 *Black Mask* and was later anthologized in A. L. Furman's *Second Mystery Companion* (1944). On April 4, 1946, *Suspense* broadcast a thirty-minute radio version starring Agnes Moorehead, and, almost simultaneously, Woolrich's story was reprinted in the June 1946 issue of *Rex Stout's Mystery Monthly*. A year or two later, as "Death Wins the Sweepstakes," the tale was included in an assortment of Woolrich material offered to newspapers by the King Features Syndicate. And finally, a thirty-minute TV film of "Post-Mortem" was aired on *Alfred Hitchcock Presents*, the evening of May 18, 1958. Arthur Hiller directed from a script by Robert C. Dennis, and the cast was headed by Joanna Moore, Fred Robbins, Steve Forrest, and James Gregory. Somehow the story has escaped being collected in any volume of Woolrich's short fiction until now.

Our final offering, "Momentum," was called "Murder Always Gathers Momentum" when it was published in the December 14, 1940, issue of *Detective Fiction Weekly*. Over the next several years, this excellent story was apparently forgotten by everyone in the genre—except the late Frederic Dannay, the editorial wizard of *Ellery Queen's Mystery Magazine*, who reprinted it in the May 1949 *EQMM* under the less unwieldy, more evocative title, which has stuck to the tale for most of its subsequent life. After its appearance in *EQMM*, the story suddenly became a media favorite. In a thirty-minute adaptation by E. Jack Neuman, it was broadcast October 27, 1949, on "radio's outstanding theater of thrills," *Suspense*, starring Victor Mature and Lurene Tuttle. Woolrich included the story in his collection *Somebody on the Phone* (1950), published by William Irish. In April 1951 it was reprinted in *Flynn's Detective Fiction Magazine* (the then current name of *Detective Fiction Weekly*, which had become a monthly) as "Murder Is a Snowball." Then the editor of *The Saint Detective Magazine*, Hans Stefan Santesson, changed the story's title to "Murder Gathers Momentum" for its appearance in that periodical's July 1954 issue. The Dannay title, "Momentum," was restored when a thirty-minute TV film version was aired June 24, 1956, on *Alfred Hitchcock Presents*. Robert Stevens directed from a script by Francis Cockrell, who was to write the teleplay for Hitchcock's haunting *Four O'Clock* a year later, and Skip Homeier and Joanne Woodward starred as the doom-stalked Paines. But this all-too-straight-forward little picture left out most of the Depression Era desperation and anguish that, as you're about to see, permeate Woolrich's story.

Two years after the last *Alfred Hitchcock Presents* half-hour based on Woolrich, Hitchcock directed what many consider the finest movie he ever made, *Psycho* (1960), based on the Robert Bloch novel of the same name. Bloch's psychopathic mass murderer, Norman Bates, was a fat, repulsive toad of a man with whom it's impossible to empathize. With the aid of a brilliant performance by Anthony Perkins, Hitchcock transformed this mother-obsessed woman-slasher into a fully human and overwhelmingly sympathetic character—young, painfully thin, and intense, eyes shadow-haunted, a man who knows in the darkness of his soul that the accident of birth has chained him forever and who is gifted or cursed with total insight into his own condition and ours.

NORMAN: I think that we're all in our private traps, clamped in them. And none of us can ever get out. We scratch and claw, but only at the air, only at each other, and for all of it we never budge an inch.
MARION: Sometimes we deliberately step into those traps.
NORMAN: I was born in mine.

Was Hitchock's Norman Bates modeled to any extent on Woolrich? The director is dead now too, and none of the dozens of film enthusiasts who interviewed him during his lifetime ever thought to ask him that question (and considering Hitchcock's notorious disinterest in the wellsprings of his own creativity, they wouldn't have gotten a straight answer if they had). But those who know the lives and work of both men might reply with a question of their own: How could he not have been?

Woolrich lived and wrote for more than a quarter century after the last of these five stories was published, and in a fragment found among his papers he explained as best he could why he wrote as he did. "I was only trying to cheat death," he said. "I was only trying to surmount for a little while the darkness that all my life I surely knew was going to come rolling in on me some day and obliterate me." In the end, of course, he had to die, as we all do. But as long as there are readers to be haunted by the fruit of his life, by the way he took his wretched psychological environment and his sense of entrapment and loneliness and turned them into poetry of the shadows, the world that Woolrich imagined lives.

REAR WINDOW

I DIDN'T KNOW THEIR names. I'd never heard their voices. I didn't even know them by sight, strictly speaking, for their faces were too small to fill in with identifiable features at that distance. Yet I could have constructed a timetable of their comings and goings, their daily habits and activities. They were the rear-window dwellers around me.

Sure, I suppose it *was* a little bit like prying, could even have been mistaken for the fevered concentration of a Peeping Tom. That wasn't my fault, that wasn't the idea. The idea was, my movements were strictly limited just around this time. I could get from the window to the bed, and from the bed to the window, and that was all. The bay window was about the best feature my rear bedroom had in the warm weather. It was unscreened, so I had to sit with the light out or I would have had every insect in the vicinity in on me. I couldn't sleep, because I was used to getting plenty of exercise. I'd never acquired the habit of reading books to ward off boredom, so I hadn't that to turn to. Well, what should I do, sit there with my eyes tightly shuttered?

Just to pick a few at random: Straight over, and the windows square, there was a young jitter-couple, kids in their teens, only just married. It would have killed them to stay home one night. They were always in such a hurry to go, wherever it was they went, they never remembered to turn out the lights. I don't think it missed once in all the time I was watching. But they never forgot altogether, either. I was to learn to call this delayed action, as you will see. He'd always come skittering madly back in about five minutes, probably from all the way down in the street, and rush around killing the switches. Then fall over something in the dark on his way out. They gave me an inward chuckle, those two.

The next house down, the windows already narrowed a little with perspective. There was a certain light in that one that always went out each night too. Something about it, it used to make me a little sad. There was a woman living there with her child, a young widow I suppose. I'd see her put the child to bed, and then bend over and kiss her in a wistful sort of way. She'd shade the light off her and sit there painting her eyes and mouth. Then she'd go out. She'd never come back till the night was nearly spent. Once I was still up, and I looked and she was sitting there motionless with her head buried in her arms. Something about it, it used to make me a little sad.

The third one down no longer offered any insight, the windows were just slits like in a medieval battlement, due to foreshortening. That brings us around to the one on the end. In that one, frontal vision came back full-depth again, since it stood at right angles to the rest, my own included, sealing up the inner hollow all these houses backed on. I could see into it, from the rounded projection of my bay window, as freely as into a doll house with its rear wall sliced away. And scaled down to about the same size.

It was a flat building. Unlike all the rest it had been constructed originally as such, not just cut up into furnished rooms. It topped them by two stories and had rear fire escapes, to show for this distinction. But it was old, evidently hadn't shown a profit. It was in the process of being modernized. Instead of clearing the entire building while the work was going on, they were doing it a flat at a time, in order to lose as little rental income as possible. Of the six rearward flats it offered to view, the topmost one had already been completed, but not yet rented. They were working on the fifth-floor one now, disturbing the peace of everyone all up and down the "inside" of the block with their hammering and sawing.

I felt sorry for the couple in the flat below. I used to wonder how they stood it with that bedlam going on above their heads. To make it worse the wife was in chronic poor health, too; I could tell that even at a distance by the listless way she moved about over there, and remained in her bathrobe without dressing. Sometimes I'd see her sitting by the window, holding her head. I used to wonder why he didn't have a doctor in to look her over, but maybe they couldn't afford it. He seemed to be out of work. Often their bedroom light was on late at night behind the drawn shade, as though she were unwell and he was sitting up with her. And one night in particular he must have had to sit up with her all night, it remained on until nearly daybreak. Not that I sat watching all that time. But the light was still burning at three in the morning, when I finally transferred from chair to bed to see if I could get a little sleep myself. And when I failed to, and hopscotched back again around dawn, it was still peering wanly out behind the tan shade.

Moments later, with the first brightening of day, it suddenly dimmed around the edges of the shade, and then shortly afterward, not that one, but a shade in one of the other rooms—for all of them alike had been down—went up, and I saw him standing there looking out.

He was holding a cigarette in his hand. I couldn't see it, but I could tell it was that by the quick, nervous little jerks with which he kept putting his hand to his mouth, and the haze I saw rising around his head. Worried about her, I guess. I didn't blame him for that. Any husband would have been. She must have only just dropped off to sleep, after night-long suffering. And then in another hour or so, at the most, that sawing of wood and clattering of buckets was going to start in over them again. Well, it wasn't any of my business, I said to myself, but he really ought to get her out of there. If I had an ill wife on my hands. . . .

He was leaning slightly out, maybe an inch past the window frame, carefully scanning the back faces of all the houses abutting on the hollow square that lay before him. You can tell, even at a distance, when a person is looking fixedly. There's something about the way the head is held. And yet his scrutiny wasn't held fixedly to any one point, it was a slow, sweeping one, moving along the houses on the opposite side from me first. When it got to the end of them, I knew it would cross over to my side and come back along there. Before it did, I withdrew several yards inside my room, to let it go safely by. I didn't want him to think I was sitting there prying into his affairs. There was still enough blue night-shade in my room to keep my slight withdrawal from catching his eye.

When I returned to my original position a moment or two later, he was gone. He had raised two more of the shades. The bedroom one was still down. I wondered vaguely why he had given that peculiar, comprehensive, semicircular stare at all the rear windows around him. There wasn't anyone at any of them, at such an hour. It wasn't important, of course. It was just a little oddity; it failed to blend in with his being worried or disturbed about his wife. When you're worried or disturbed, that's an internal preoccupation, you stare vacantly at nothing at all. When you stare around you in a great sweeping arc at windows, that betrays external preoccupation, outward interest. One doesn't quite jibe with the other. To call such a discrepancy trifling is to add to its importance. Only someone like me, stewing in a vacuum of total idleness, would have noticed it at all.

The flat remained lifeless after that, as far as could be judged by its windows. He must have either gone out or gone to bed himself. Three of the shades remained at normal height, the one masking the bedroom remained down. Sam, my day houseman, came in not long after with my eggs and morning paper, and I had that to kill time with for awhile. I stopped thinking about other people's windows and staring at them.

The sun slanted down on one side of the hollow oblong all morning long, then it shifted over to the other side for the afternoon. Then it started to slip off both alike, and it was evening again—another day gone.

The lights started to come on around the quadrangle. Here and there a wall played back, like a sounding board, a snatch of radio program that was coming in too loud. If you listened carefully you could hear an occasional click of dishes mixed in, faint, far off. The chain of little habits that were their lives unreeled themselves. They were all bound in them tighter than the tightest straitjacket any jailer ever devised, though they all thought themselves free. The jitterbugs made their nightly dash for the great open spaces, forgot their lights, he came careening back, thumbed them out, and their place was dark until the early morning hours. The woman put her child to bed, leaned mournfully over its cot, then sat down with heavy despair to redden her mouth.

In the fourth-floor flat at right angles to the long, interior "street" the three shades had remained up, and the fourth shade had remained at full length, all day long. I hadn't been conscious of that because I hadn't particularly been looking at it, or thinking of it, until now. My eyes may have rested on those windows at times, during the day, but my thoughts had been elsewhere. It was only when a light suddenly went up in the

end room behind one of the raised shades, which was
their kitchen, that I realized that the shades had been
untouched like that all day. That also brought something
else to my mind that hadn't been in it until now: I hadn't
seen the woman all day. I hadn't seen any sign of life
within those windows until now.

He'd come in from outside. The entrance was at the
opposite side of their kitchen, away from the window.
He'd left his hat on, so I knew he'd just come in from the
outside.

He didn't remove his hat. As though there was no one
there to remove it for any more. Instead, he pushed it
farther to the back of his head by pronging a hand to the
roots of his hair. That gesture didn't denote removal of
perspiration, I knew. To do that a person makes a sidewise sweep—this was up over his forehead. It indicated
some sort of harassment or uncertainty. Besides, if he'd
been suffering from excess warmth, the first thing he
would have done would be to take off his hat altogether.

She didn't come out to greet him. The first link, of the
so-strong chain of habits, of custom, that binds us all,
had snapped wide open.

She must be so ill she had remained in bed, in the
room behind the lowered shade, all day. I watched. He
remained where he was, two rooms away from there.
Expectancy became surprise, surprise incomprehension.
Funny, I thought, that he doesn't go in to her. Or at least
go as far as the doorway, look in to see how she is.

Maybe she was asleep, and he didn't want to disturb
her. Then immediately: but how can he know for sure
that she's asleep, without at least looking in at her? He
just came in himself.

He came forward and stood there by the window, as
he had at dawn. Sam had carried out my tray quite some
time before, and my lights were out. I held my ground, I
knew he couldn't see me within the darkness of the bay

window. He stood there motionless for several minutes. And now his attitude was the proper one for inner preoccupation. He stood there looking downward at nothing, lost in thought.

He's worried about her, I said to myself, as any man would be. It's the most natural thing in the world. Funny, though, he should leave her in the dark like that, without going near her. If he's worried, then why didn't he at least look in on her on returning? Here was another of those trivial discrepancies, between inward motivation and outward indication. And just as I was thinking that, the original one, that I had noted at daybreak, repeated itself. His head went up with renewed alertness, and I could see it start to give that slow circular sweep of interrogation around the panorama of rearward windows again. True, the light was behind him this time, but there was enough of it falling on him to show me the microscopic but continuous shift of direction his head made in the process. I remained carefully immobile until the distant glance had passed me safely by. Motion attracts.

Why is he so interested in other people's windows, I wondered detachedly. And of course an effective brake to dwell on that thought too lingeringly clamped down almost at once: Look who's talking. What about you yourself?

An important difference escaped me. I wasn't worried about anything. He, presumably, was.

Down came the shades again. The lights stayed on behind their beige opaqueness. But behind the one that had remained down all along, the room remained dark.

Time went by. Hard to say how much—a quarter of an hour, twenty minutes. A cricket chirped in one of the back yards. Sam came in to see if I wanted anything before he went home for the night. I told him no, I didn't—it was all right, run along. He stood there for a minute, head down. Then I saw him shake it slightly, as if at something he didn't like. "What's the matter?" I asked.

"You know what that means? My old mammy told it to me, and she never told me a lie in her life. I never once seen it to miss, either."

"What, the cricket?"

"Any time you hear one of them things, that's a sign of death—someplace close around."

I swept the back of my hand at him. "Well, it isn't in here, so don't let it worry you."

He went out, muttering stubbornly: "It's somewhere close by, though. Somewhere not very far off. Got to be."

The door closed after him, and I stayed there alone in the dark.

It was a stifling night, much closer than the one before. I could hardly get a breath of air even by the open window at which I sat. I wondered how he—that unknown over there—could stand it behind those drawn shades.

Then suddenly, just as idle speculation about this whole matter was about to alight on some fixed point in my mind, crystallize into something like suspicion, up came the shades again, and off it flitted, as formless as ever and without having had a chance to come to rest on anything.

He was in the middle windows, the living room. He'd taken off his coat and shirt, was bare-armed in his undershirt. He hadn't been able to stand it himself, I guess—the sultriness.

I couldn't make out what he was doing at first. He seemed to be busy in a perpendicular, up-and-down way rather than lengthwise. He remained in one place, but he kept dipping down out of sight and then straightening up into view again, at irregular intervals. It was almost like some sort of calisthenic exercise, except that the dips and rises weren't evenly timed enough for that. Sometimes he'd stay down a long time, sometimes he'd bob right up again, sometimes he'd go down two or three times in rapid succession. There was some sort of a widespread black V railing him off from the window. Whatever it was, there was just a sliver of it showing above the upward inclination to which the window sill deflected my line of vision. All it did was strike off the bottom of his undershirt, to the extent of a sixteenth of an inch maybe. But I haven't seen it there at other times, and I couldn't tell what it was.

Suddenly he left it for the first time since the shades had gone up, came out around it to the outside, stooped down into another part of the room, and straightened again with an armful of what looked like varicolored pennants at the distance at which I was. He went back behind the V and allowed them to fall across the top of it for a moment, and stay that way. He made one of his dips down out of sight and stayed that way a good while.

The "pennants" slung across the V kept changing color right in front of my eyes. I have very good sight. One moment they were white, the next red, the next blue.

Then I got it. They were a woman's dresses, and he was pulling them down to him one by one, taking the topmost one each time. Suddenly they were all gone, the V was black and bare again, and his torso had reappeared. I knew what it was now, and what he was doing. The dresses had told me. He confirmed it for me. He spread his arms to the ends of the V, I could see him heave and hitch, as if exerting pressure, and suddenly the V had folded up, become a cubed wedge. Then he made rolling motions with his whole upper body, and the wedge disappeared off to one side.

He'd been packing a trunk, packing his wife's things into a large upright trunk.

He reappeared at the kitchen window presently, stood still for a moment. I saw him draw his arm across his forehead, not once but several times, and then whip the

end of it off into space. Sure, it was hot work for such a
night. Then he reached up along the wall and took something down. Since it was the kitchen he was in, my imagi-
nation had to supply a cabinet and a bottle.

I could see the two or three quick passes his hand
made to his mouth after that. I said to myself tolerantly:
That's what nine men out of ten would do after packing
a trunk—take a good stiff drink. And if the tenth didn't,
it would only be because he didn't have any liquor at
hand.

Then he came closer to the window again, and standing edgewise to the side of it, so that only a thin paring of
his head and shoulder showed, peered watchfully out
into the dark quadrilateral, along the line of windows,
most of them unlighted by now, once more. He always
started on the left-hand side, the side opposite mine, and
made his circuit of inspection from there on around.

That was the second time in one evening I'd seen him
do that. And once at daybreak, made three times altogether. I smiled mentally. You'd almost think he felt
guilty about something. It was probably nothing, just an
odd little habit, a quirk, that he didn't know he had
himself. I had them myself, everyone does.

He withdrew into the room, and it blacked out. His
figure passed into the one that was still lighted next to it,
the living room. That blacked next. It didn't surprise me
that the third room, the bedroom with the drawn shade,
didn't light up on his entering there. He wouldn't want to
disturb her, of course—particularly if she was going
away tomorrow for her health, as his packing of her
trunk showed. She needed all the rest she could get,
before making the trip. Simple enough for him to slip
into bed in the dark.

It did surprise me, though, when a match-flare winked
some time later, to have it still come from the darkened
living room. He must be lying down in there, trying to
sleep on a sofa or something for the night. He hadn't

gone near the bedroom at all, was staying out of it altogether. That puzzled me, frankly. That was carrying
solicitude almost too far.

Ten minutes or so later, there was another match-
wink, still from that same living room window. He
couldn't sleep.

The night brooded down on both of us alike, the
curiosity-monger in the bay window, the chain-smoker
in the fourth-floor flat, without giving any answer. The
only sound was that interminable cricket.

I was back at the window again with the first sun of
morning. Not because of him. My mattress was like a
bed of hot coals. Sam found me there when he came in to
get things ready for me. "You're going to be a wreck, Mr.
Jeff," was all he said.

First, for awhile, there was no sign of life over there.
Then suddenly I saw his head bob up from somewhere
down out of sight in the living room, so I knew I'd been
right; he'd spent the night on a sofa or easy chair in
there. Now, of course, he'd look in at her, to see how she
was, find out if she felt any better. That was only common ordinary humanity. He hadn't been near her, so far
as I could make out, since two nights before.

He didn't. He dressed, and he went in the opposite
direction, into the kitchen, and wolfed something in
there, standing up and using both hands. Then he suddenly turned and moved off side, in the direction in
which I knew the flat-entrance to be, as if he had just
heard some summons, like the doorbell.

Sure enough, in a moment he came back, and there
were two men with him in leather aprons. Expressmen. I
saw him standing by while they laboriously maneuvered
that cubed black wedge out between them, in the direction
they'd just come from. He did more than just stand by. He
practically hovered over them, kept shifting from side to
side, he was so anxious to see that it was done right.

Then he came back alone, and I saw him swipe his arm

across his head, as though it was he, not they, who was all heated up from the effort.

So he was forwarding her trunk, to wherever it was she was going. That was all.

He reached up along the wall again and took something down. He was taking another drink. Two. Three. I said to myself, a little at a loss: Yes, but he hasn't just packed a trunk this time. That trunk has been standing packed and ready since last night. Where does the hard work come in? The sweat and the need for a bracer?

Now, at last, after all those hours, he finally did go in to her. I saw his form pass through the living room and go beyond, into the bedroom. Up went the shade, that had been down all this time. Then he turned his head and looked around behind him. In a certain way, a way that was unmistakable, even from where I was. Not in one certain direction, as one looks at a person. But from side to side, and up and down, and all around, as one looks at—*an empty room*.

He stepped back, bent a little, gave a fling of his arms, and an unoccupied mattress and bedding upended over the foot of a bed, stayed that way, emptily curved. A second one followed a moment later.

She wasn't in there.

They use the expression "delayed action." I found out then what it meant. For two days a sort of formless uneasiness, a disembodied suspicion, I don't know what to call it, had been flitting and volplaning around in my mind, like an insect looking for a landing place. More than once, just as it had been ready to settle, some slight thing, some slight reassuring thing, such as the raising of the shades after they had been down unnaturally long, had been enough to keep it winging aimlessly, prevent it from staying still long enough for me to recognize it. The point of contact had been there all along, waiting to receive it. Now, for some reason, within a split second

after he tossed over the empty mattresses, it landed—
zoom! And the point of contact expanded—or exploded,
whatever you care to call it—into a certainty of murder.

In other words, the rational part of my mind was far
behind the instinctive, subconscious part. Delayed action. Now the one had caught up to the other. The
thought-message that sparked from the synchronization
was: He's done something to her!

I looked down and my hand was bunching the goods
over my kneecap, it was knotted so tight. I forced it to
open. I said to myself, steadyingly: Now wait a minute,
be careful, go slow. You've seen nothing. You know
nothing. You only have the negative proof that you don't
see her any more.

Sam was standing there looking over at me from the
pantryway. He said accusingly: "You ain't touched a
thing. And your face looks like a sheet."

It felt like one. It had that needling feeling, when the
blood has left it involuntarily. It was more to get him out
of the way and give myself some elbow room for undisturbed thinking, than anything else, that I said: "Sam,
what's the street address of that building down there?
Don't stick your head too far out and gape at it."

"Somep'n or other Benedict Avenue." He scratched
his neck helpfully.

"I know that. Chase around the corner a minute and
get me the exact number on it, will you?"

"Why you want to know that for?" he asked as he
turned to go.

"None of your business," I said with the good-natured
firmness that was all that was necessary to take care of
that once and for all. I called after him just as he was
closing the door: "And while you're about it, step into
the entrance and see if you can tell from the mail-
boxes who has the fourth-floor rear. Don't get me the
wrong one now. And try not to let anyone catch you
at it."

He went out mumbling something that sounded like, "When a man ain't got nothing to do but just sit all day, he sure can think up the blamest things ——" The door closed and I settled down to some good constructive thinking.

I said to myself: What are you really building up this monstrous supposition on? Let's see what you've got. Only that there were several little things wrong with the mechanism, the chain-belt, of their recurrent daily habits over there. 1. The lights were on all night the first night. 2. He came in later than usual the second night. 3. He left his hat on. 4. She didn't come out to greet him—she hasn't appeared since the evening before the lights were on all night. 5. He took a drink after he finished packing her trunk. But he took three stiff drinks the next morning, immediately after her trunk went out. 6. He was inwardly disturbed and worried, yet superimposed upon this was an unnatural external concern about the surrounding rear windows that was off-key. 7. He slept in the living room, didn't go near the bedroom, during the night before the departure of the trunk.

Very well. If she had been ill that first night, and he had sent her away for her health, that automatically canceled out points 1, 2, 3, 4. It left points 5 and 6 totally unimportant and unincriminating. But when it came up against 7, I hit a stumbling block.

If she went away immediately after being ill that first night, why didn't he want to sleep in their bedroom *last night?* Sentiment? Hardly. Two perfectly good beds in one room, only a sofa or uncomfortable easy chair in the other. Why should he stay out of there if she was already gone? Just because he missed her, was lonely? A grown man doesn't act that way. All right, then she was still in there.

Sam came back parenthetically at this point and said: "That house is Number 525 Benedict Avenue. The fourth-floor rear, it got the name of Mr. and Mrs. Lars Thorwald up."

"Sh-h," I silenced, and motioned him backhand out of my ken.

"First he wants it, then he don't," he grumbled philosophically, and retired to his duties.

I went ahead digging at it. But if she was still in there, in that bedroom last night, then she couldn't have gone away to the country, because I never saw her leave today. She could have left without my seeing her in the early hours of yesterday morning. I'd missed a few hours, been asleep. But this morning I had been up before he was himself, I only saw his head rear up from the sofa after I'd been at the window for some time.

To go at all she would have had to go yesterday morning. Then why had he left the bedroom shade down, left the mattresses undisturbed, until today? Above all, why had he stayed out of that room last night? That was evidence that she hadn't gone, was still in there. Then today, immediately after the trunk had been dispatched, he went in, pulled up the shade, tossed·over the mattresses, and showed that she hadn't been in there. The thing was like a crazy spiral.

No, it wasn't either. *Immediately after the trunk had been dispatched*——

The trunk.

That did it.

I looked around to make sure the door was safely closed between Sam and me. My hand hovered uncertainly over the telephone dial a minute. Boyne, he'd be the one to tell about it. He was on Homicide. He had been, anyway, when I'd last seen him. I didn't want to get a flock of strange dicks and cops into my hair. I didn't want to be involved any more than I had to. Or at all, if possible.

They switched my call to the right place after a couple of wrong tries, and I got him finally.

"Look, Boyne? This is Hal Jeffries——"

"Well, where've you been the last sixty-two years?" he started to enthuse.

"We can take that up later. What I want you to do now is take down a name and address. Ready? Lars Thorwald. Five twenty-five Benedict Avenue. Fourth-floor rear. Got it?"

"Fourth-floor rear. Got it. What's it for?"

"Investigation. I've got a firm belief you'll uncover a murder there if you start digging at it. Don't call on me for anything more than that—just a conviction. There's been a man and wife living there until now. Now there's just the man. Her trunk went out early this morning. If you can find someone who saw *her* leave herself——"

Marshaled aloud like that and conveyed to somebody else, a lieutenant of detectives above all, it did sound flimsy, even to me. He said hesitantly, "Well, but——" Then he accepted it as was. Because I was the source. I even left my window out of it completely. I could do that with him and get away with it because he'd known me years, he didn't question my reliability. I didn't want my room all cluttered up with dicks and cops taking turns nosing out of the window in this hot weather. Let them tackle it from the front.

"Well, we'll see what we see," he said. "I'll keep you posted."

I hung up and sat back to watch and wait events. I had a grandstand seat. Or rather a grandstand seat in reverse. I could only see from behind the scenes, but not from the front. I couldn't watch Boyne go to work. I could only see the results, when and if there were any.

Nothing happened for the next few hours. The police work that I knew must be going on was as invisible as police work should be. The figure in the fourth-floor windows over there remained in sight, alone and undisturbed. He didn't go out. He was restless, roamed from room to room without staying in one place very long, but he stayed in. Once I saw him eating again—sitting down this time—and once he shaved, and once he even tried to read the paper, but he didn't stay with it long.

Little unseen wheels were in motion around him. Small and harmless as yet, preliminaries. If he knew, I wondered to myself, would he remain there quiescent like that, or would he try to bolt out and flee? That mightn't depend so much upon his guilt as upon his sense of immunity, his feeling that he could outwit them. Of his guilt I myself was already convinced, or I wouldn't have taken the step I had.

At three my phone rang. Boyne calling back. "Jeffries? Well, I don't know. Can't you give me a little more than just a bald statement like that?"

"Why?" I fenced. "Why do I have to?"

"I've had a man over there making inquiries. I've just had his report. The building superintendent and several of the neighbors all agree she left for the country, to try and regain her health, early yesterday morning."

"Wait a minute. Did any of them *see* her leave, according to your man?"

"No."

"Then all you've gotten is a second-hand version of an unsupported statement by him. Not an eyewitness account."

"He was met returning from the depot, after he'd bought her ticket and seen her off on the train."

"That's still an unsupported statement, once removed."

"I've sent a man down there to the station to try and check with the ticket agent if possible. After all, he should have been fairly conspicuous at that early hour. And we're keeping him under observation, of course, in

the meantime, watching all his movements. The first
chance we get we're going to jump in and search the
place."

I had a feeling that they wouldn't find anything, even if
they did.

"Don't expect anything more from me. I've dropped it
in your lap. I've given you all I have to give. A name, an
address, and an opinion."

"Yes, and I've always valued your opinion highly before now, Jeff——"

"But now you don't, that it?"

"Not at all. The thing is, we haven't turned up anything that seems to bear out your impression so far."

"You haven't gotten very far along, so far."

He went back to his previous cliché. "Well, we'll see
what we see. Let you know later."

Another hour or so went by, and sunset came on. I
saw him start to get ready to go out, over there. He put
on his hat, put his hand in his pocket and stood still
looking at it for a minute. Counting change, I guess. It
gave me a peculiar sense of suppressed excitement,
knowing they were going to come in the minute he left. I
thought grimly, as I saw him take a last look around: If
you've got anything to hide, brother, now's the time to
hide it.

He left. A breath-holding interval of misleading emp-
tiness descended on the flat. A three-alarm fire couldn't
have pulled my eyes off those windows. Suddenly the
door by which he had just left parted slightly and two
men insinuated themselves, one behind the other. There
they were now. They closed it behind them, separated at
once, and got busy. One took the bedroom, one the
kitchen, and they started to work their way toward one
another again from those extremes of the flat. They were
thorough. I could see them going over everything from
top to bottom. They took the living room together. One
cased one side, the other man the other.

They'd already finished before the warning caught them. I could tell that by the way they straightened up and stood facing one another frustratedly for a minute. Then both their heads turned sharply, as at a tip-off by doorbell that he was coming back. They got out fast.

I wasn't unduly disheartened, I'd expected that. My own feeling all along had been that they wouldn't find anything incriminating around. The trunk had gone.

He came in with a mountainous brown-paper bag sitting in the curve of one arm. I watched him closely to see if he'd discover that someone had been there in his absence. Apparently he didn't. They'd been adroit about it.

He stayed in the rest of the night. Sat tight, safe and sound. He did some desultory drinking, I could see him sitting there by the window and his hand would hoist every once in awhile, but not to excess. Apparently everything was under control, the tension had eased, now that—the trunk was out.

Watching him across the night, I speculated: Why doesn't he get out? If I'm right about him, and I am, why does he stick around—after it? That brought its own answer: Because he doesn't know anyone's on to him yet. He doesn't think there's any hurry. To go too soon, right after she has, would be more dangerous than to stay awhile.

The night wore on. I sat there waiting for Boyne's call. It came later than I thought it would. I picked the phone up in the dark. He was getting ready to go to bed, over there, now. He'd risen from where he'd been sitting drinking in the kitchen, and put the light out. He went into the living room, lit that. He started to pull his shirt-tail up out of his belt. Boyne's voice was in my ear as my eyes were on him, over there. Three-cornered arrangement.

"Hello, Jeff? Listen, absolutely nothing. We searched the place while he was out——"

I nearly said, "I know you did, I saw it," but checked myself in time.

"—and didn't turn up a thing. But ——" He stopped as though this was going to be important. I waited impatiently for him to go ahead.

"Downstairs in his letter box we found a post card waiting for him. We fished it up out of the slot with bent pins ——"

"And?"

"And it was from his wife, written only yesterday from some farm up-country. Here's the message we copied: 'Arrived O. K. Already feeling a little better. Love, Anna.'"

I said, faintly but stubbornly: "You say, written only yesterday. Have you proof of that? What was the postmark-date on it?"

He made a disgusted sound down in his tonsils. At me, not it. "The postmark was blurred. A corner of it got wet, and the ink smudged."

"All of it blurred?"

"The year-date," he admitted. "The hour and the month came out O. K. August. And seven thirty P.M., it was mailed at."

This time I made the disgusted sound, in my larynx. "August, seven thirty P.M.—1937 or 1939 or 1942. You have no proof how it got into that mail box, whether it came from a letter carrier's pouch or from the back of some bureau drawer!"

"Give up, Jeff," he said. "There's such a thing as going too far."

I don't know what I would have said. That is, if I hadn't happened to have my eyes on the Thorwald flat living room windows just then. Probably very little. The post card *had* shaken me, whether I admitted it or not. But I was looking over there. The light had gone out as soon as he'd taken his shirt off. But the bedroom didn't light up. A match-flare winked from the living room, low down, as from an easy chair or sofa. With two unused beds in the bedroom, he was *still staying out of there*.

"Boyne," I said in a glassy voice, "I don't care what post cards from the other world you've turned up, I say that man has done away with his wife! Trace that trunk he shipped out. Open it up when you've located it—and I think you'll find her!"

And I hung up without waiting to hear what he was going to do about it. He didn't ring back, so I suspected he was going to give my suggestion a spin after all, in spite of his loudly proclaimed skepticism.

I stayed there by the window all night, keeping a sort of death-watch. There were two more match-flares after the first, at about half-hour intervals. Nothing more after that. So possibly he was asleep over there. Possibly not. I had to sleep some myself, and I finally succumbed in the flaming light of the early sun. Anything that he was going to do, he would have done under cover of darkness and not waited for broad daylight. There wouldn't be anything much to watch, for a while now. And what was there that he needed to do any more, anyway? Nothing, just sit tight and let a little disarming time slip by.

It seemed like five minutes later that Sam came over and touched me, but it was already high noon. I said irritably: "Didn't you lamp that note I pinned up, for you to let me sleep?"

He said: "Yeah, but it's your old friend Inspector Boyne. I figured you'd sure want to——"

It was a personal visit this time. Boyne came into the room behind him without waiting, and without much cordiality.

I said to get rid of Sam: "Go inside and smack a couple of eggs together."

Boyne began in a galvanized-iron voice: "Jeff, what do you mean by doing anything like this to me? I've made a fool out of myself thanks to you. Sending my men out right and left on wild-goose chases. Thank God, I didn't put my foot in it any worse than I did, and have this guy picked up and brought in for questioning."

"Oh, then you don't think that's necessary?" I suggested, dryly.

The look he gave me took care of that. "I'm not alone in the department, you know. There are men over me I'm accountable to for my actions. That looks great, don't it, sending one of my fellows one-half-a-day's train ride up into the sticks to some God-forsaken whistle-stop or other at departmental expense——"

"Then you located the trunk?"

"We traced it through the express agency," he said flintily.

"And you opened it?"

"We did better than that. We got in touch with the various farmhouses in the immediate locality, and Mrs. Thornwald came down to the junction in a produce-truck from one of them and opened it for him herself, with her own keys!"

Very few men have ever gotten a look from an old friend such as I got from him. At the door he said, stiff as a rifle barrel: "Just let's forget all about it, shall we? That's about the kindest thing either one of us can do for the other. You're not yourself, and I'm out a little of my own pocket money, time and temper. Let's let it go at that. If you want to telephone me in future I'll be glad to give you my home number."

The door went *whopp!* behind him.

For about ten minutes after he stormed out my numbed mind was in a sort of straitjacket. Then it started to wriggle its way free. The hell with the police. I can't prove it to them, maybe, but I can prove it to myself, one way or the other, once and for all. Either I'm wrong or I'm right. He's got his armor on against them. But his back is naked and unprotected against me.

I called Sam in. "Whatever became of that spyglass we

used to have, when we were bumming around on that cabin-cruiser that season?"

He found it some place downstairs and came in with it, blowing on it and rubbing it along his sleeve. I let it lie idle in my lap first. I took a piece of paper and a pencil and wrote six words on it: *What have you done with her?*

I sealed it in an envelope and left the envelope blank. I said to Sam: "Now here's what I want you to do, and I want you to be slick about it. You take this, go in that building 525, climb the stairs to the fourth-floor rear, and ease it under the door. You're fast, at least you used to be. Let's see if you're fast enough to keep from being caught at it. Then when you get safely down again, give the outside doorbell a little poke, to attract attention."

His mouth started to open.

"And don't ask me any questions, you understand? I'm not fooling."

He went, and I got the spyglass ready.

I got him in the right focus after a minute or two. A face leaped up, and I was really seeing him for the first time. Dark-haired, but unmistakable Scandinavian ancestry. Looked like a sinewy customer, although he didn't run to much bulk.

About five minutes went by. His head turned sharply, profilewards. That was the bell-poke, right there. The note must be in already.

He gave me the back of his head as he went back toward the flat-door. The lens could follow him all the way to the rear, where my unaided eyes hadn't been able to before.

He opened the door first, missed seeing it, looked out on a level. He closed it. Then dipped, straightened up. He had it. I could see him turning it this way and that.

He shifted in, away from the door, nearer the window. He thought danger lay near the door, safety away from it. He didn't know it was the other way around, the deeper into his own rooms he retreated the greater the danger.

He'd torn it open, he was reading it. God, how I watched his expression. My eyes clung to it like leeches. There was a sudden widening, a pulling—the whole skin of his face seemed to stretch back behind the ears, narrowing his eyes to Mongoloids. Shock. Panic. His hand pushed out and found the wall, and he braced himself with it. Then he went back toward the door again slowly. I could see him creeping up on it, stalking it as though it were something alive. He opened it so slenderly you couldn't see it at all, peered fearfully through the crack. Then he closed it, and he came back, zigzag, off balance from sheer reflex dismay. He toppled into a chair and snatched up a drink. Out of the bottle neck itself this time. And even while he was holding it to his lips, his head was turned looking over his shoulder at the door that had suddenly thrown his secret in his face.

I put the glass down.

Guilty! Guilty as all hell, and the police be damned!

My hand started toward the phone, came back again. What was the use? They wouldn't listen now any more than they had before. "You should have seen his face, etc." And I could hear Boyne's answer: "Anyone gets a jolt from an anonymous letter, true or false. You would yourself." They had a real live Mrs. Thorwald to show me—or thought they had. I'd have to show them the dead one, to prove that they both weren't one and the same. I, from my window, had to show them a body.

Well, he'd have to show me first.

It took hours before I got it. I kept pegging away at it, pegging away at it, while the afternoon wore away. Meanwhile he was pacing back and forth there like a caged panther. Two minds with but one thought, turned inside-out in my case. How to keep it hidden, how to see that it wasn't kept hidden.

I was afraid he might try to light out, but if he

intended doing that he was going to wait until after dark, apparently, so I had a little time yet. Possibly he didn't want to himself, unless he was driven to it—still felt that it was more dangerous than to stay.

The customary sights and sounds around me went on unnoticed, while the main stream of my thoughts pounded like a torrent against that one obstacle stubbornly damming them up: how to get him to give the location away to me, so that I could give it away in turn to the police.

I was dimly conscious, I remember, of the landlord or somebody bringing in a prospective tenant to look at the sixth-floor apartment, the one that had already been finished. This was two over Thorwald's; they were still at work on the in-between one. At one point an odd little bit of synchronization, completely accidental of course, cropped up. Landlord and tenant both happened to be near the living room windows on the sixth at the same moment that Thorwald was near those on the fourth. Both parties moved onward simultaneously into the kitchen from there, and, passing the blind spot of the wall, appeared next at the kitchen windows. It was uncanny, they were almost like precision-strollers or puppets manipulated on one and the same string. It probably wouldn't have happened again just like that in another fifty years. Immediately afterwards they digressed, never to repeat themselves like that again.

The thing was, something about it had disturbed me. There had been some slight flaw or hitch to mar its smoothness. I tried for a moment or two to figure out what it had been, and couldn't. The landlord and tenant had gone now, and only Thorwald was in sight. My unaided memory wasn't enough to recapture it for me. My eyesight might have if it had been repeated, but it wasn't.

It sank into my subconscious, to ferment there like yeast, while I went back to the main problem at hand.

I got it finally. It was well after dark, but I finally hit on a way. It mightn't work, it was cumbersome and roundabout, but it was the only way I could think of. An alarmed turn of the head, a quick precautionary step in one certain direction, was all I needed. And to get this brief, flickering, transitory give-away, I needed two phone calls and an absence of about half an hour on his part between them.

I leafed a directory by matchlight until I'd found what I wanted: *Thorwald, Lars. 525 Bndct. . . . SWansea 5-2114.*

I blew out the match, picked up the phone in the dark. It was like television. I could see to the other end of my call, only not along the wire but by a direct channel of vision from window to window.

He said "Hullo?" gruffly.

I thought: How strange this is. I've been accusing him of murder for three days straight, and only now I'm hearing his voice for the first time.

I didn't try to disguise my own voice. After all, he'd never see me and I'd never see him. I said: "You got my note?"

He said guardedly: "Who is this?"

"Just somebody who happens to know."

He said craftily: "Know what?"

"Know what you know. You and I, we're the only ones."

He controlled himself well. I didn't hear a sound. But he didn't know he was open another way too. I had the glass balanced there at proper height on two large books on the sill. Through the window I saw him pull open the collar of his shirt as though its stricture was intolerable. Then he backed his hand over his eyes like you do when there's a light blinding you.

His voice came back firmly. "I don't know what you're talking about."

"Business, that's what I'm talking about. It should be

worth something to me, shouldn't it? To keep it from going any further." I wanted to keep him from catching on that it was the windows. I still needed them, I needed them now more than ever. "You weren't very careful about your door the other night. Or maybe the draft swung it open a little."

That hit him where he lived. Even the stomach-heave reached me over the wire. "You didn't see anything. There wasn't anything to see."

"That's up to you. Why should I go to the police?" I coughed a little. "If it would pay me not to."

"Oh," he said. And there was relief of a sort in it. "D'you want to—see me? Is that it?"

"That would be the best way, wouldn't it? How much can you bring with you for now?"

"I've only got about seventy dollars around here."

"All right, then we can arrange the rest for later. Do you know where Lakeside Park is? I'm near there now. Suppose we make it there." That was about thirty minutes away. Fifteen there and fifteen back. "There's a little pavilion as you go in."

"How many of you are there?" he asked cautiously.

"Just me. It pays to keep things to yourself. That way you don't have to divvy up."

He seemed to like that too. "I'll take a run out," he said, "just to see what it's all about."

I watched him more closely than ever, after he'd hung up. He flitted straight through to the end room, the bedroom, that he didn't go near any more. He disappeared into a clothes-closet in there, stayed a minute, came out again. He must have taken something out of a hidden cranny or niche in there that even the dicks had missed. I could tell by the piston-like motion of his hand, just before it disappeared inside his coat, what it was. A gun.

It's a good thing, I thought, I'm not out there in Lakeside Park waiting for my seventy dollars.

The place blacked and he was on his way.

I called Sam in. "I want you to do something for me that's a little risky. In fact, damn risky. You might break a leg, or you might get shot, or you might even get pinched. We've been together ten years, and I wouldn't ask you anything like that if I could do it myself. But I can't, and it's got to be done." Then I told him. "Go out the back way, cross the back yard fences, and see if you can get into that fourth-floor flat up the fire escape. He's left one of the windows down a little from the top."

"What do you want me to look for?"

"Nothing." The police had been there already, so what was the good of that? "There are three rooms over there. I want you to disturb everything just a little bit, in all three, to show someone's been in there. Turn up the edge of each rug a little, shift every chair and table around a little, leave the closet doors standing out. Don't pass up a thing. Here, keep your eyes on this." I took off my own wrist watch, strapped it on him. "You've got twenty-five minutes, starting from now. If you stay within those twenty-five minutes, nothing will happen to you. When you see they're up, don't wait any longer, get out and get out fast."

"Climb back down?"

"No." He wouldn't remember, in his excitement, if he'd left the windows up or not. And I didn't want him to connect danger with the back of his place, but with the front. I wanted to keep my own window out of it. "Latch the window down tight, let yourself out the door, and beat it out of the building the front way, for your life!"

"I'm just an easy mark for you," he said ruefully, but he went.

He came out through our own basement door below me, and scrambled over the fences. If anyone had challenged him from one of the surrounding windows, I was going to backstop for him, explain I'd sent him down to look for something. But no one did. He made it pretty good for anyone his age. He isn't so young any more.

Even the fire escape backing the flat, which was drawn up short, he managed to contact by standing up on something. He got in, lit the light, looked over at me. I motioned him to go ahead, not weaken.

I watched him at it. There wasn't any way I could protect him, now that he was in there. Even Thorwald would be within his rights in shooting him down—this was break and entry. I had to stay in back behind the scenes, like I had been all along. I couldn't get out in front of him as a lookout and shield him. Even the dicks had had a lookout posted.

He must have been tense, doing it. I was twice as tense, watching him do it. The twenty-five minutes took fifty to go by. Finally he came over to the window, latched it fast. The lights went, and he was out. He'd made it. I blew out a bellyful of breath that was twenty-five minutes old.

I heard him keying the street door, and when he came up I said warningly: "Leave the light out in here. Go and build yourself a great big two-story whisky punch; you're as close to white as you'll ever be."

Thorwald came back twenty-nine minutes after he'd left for Lakeside Park. A pretty slim margin to hang a man's life on. So now for the finale of the long-winded business, and here was hoping. I got my second phone call in before he had time to notice anything amiss. It was tricky timing but I'd been sitting there with the receiver ready in my hand, dialing the number over and over, then killing it each time. He came in on the 2 of 5-2114, and I saved that much time. The ring started before his hand came away from the light switch.

This was the one that was going to tell the story.

"You were supposed to bring money, not a gun; that's why I didn't show up." I saw the jolt that threw him. The window still had to stay out of it. "I saw you tap the inside of your coat, where you had it, as you came out on the street." Maybe he hadn't, but he wouldn't remember by now whether he had or not. You usually do when you're packing a gun and aren't an habitual carrier.

"Too bad you had your trip out and back for nothing. I didn't waste my time while you were gone, though. I know more now than I knew before." This was the important part. I had the glass up and I was practically fluoroscoping him. "I've found out where—it is. You know what I mean. I know now where you've got—it. I was there while you were out."

Not a word. Just quick breathing.

"Don't you believe me? Look around. Put the receiver down and take a look for yourself. I found it."

He put it down, moved as far as the living room entrance, and touched off the lights. He just looked around him once, in a sweeping, all-embracing stare, that didn't come to a head on any one fixed point, didn't center at all.

He was smiling grimly when he came back to the phone. All he said, softly and with malignant satisfaction, was: "You're a liar."

Then I saw him lay the receiver down and take his hand off it. I hung up at my end.

The test had failed. And yet it hadn't. He hadn't given the location away as I'd hoped he would. And yet that "You're a liar" was a tacit admission that it was there to be found, somewhere around him, somewhere on those premises. In such a good place that he didn't have to worry about it, didn't even have to look to make sure.

So there was a kind of sterile victory in my defeat. But it wasn't worth a damn to me.

He was standing there with his back to me, and I couldn't see what he was doing. I knew the phone was somewhere in front of him, but I thought he was just standing there pensive behind it. His head was slightly lowered, that was all. I'd hung up at my end. I didn't even see his elbow move. And if his index finger did, I couldn't see it.

He stood like that a moment or two, then finally he moved aside. The lights went out over there; I lost him. He was careful not even to strike matches, like he sometimes did in the dark.

My mind no longer distracted by having him to look at, I turned to trying to recapture something else—that troublesome little hitch in synchronization that had occurred this afternoon, when the renting agent and he both moved simultaneously from one window to the next. The closest I could get was this: it was like when you're looking at someone through a pane of imperfect glass, and a flaw in the glass distorts the symmetry of the reflected image for a second, until it has gone on past that point. Yet that wouldn't do, that was not it. The windows had been open and there had been no glass between. And I hadn't been using the lens at the time.

My phone rang. Boyne, I supposed. It wouldn't be anyone else at this hour. Maybe, after reflecting on the way he'd jumped all over me— I said "Hello" unguardedly, in my own normal voice.

There wasn't any answer.

I said: "Hello? Hello? Hello?" I kept giving away samples of my voice.

There wasn't a sound from first to last.

I hung up finally. It was still dark over there, I noticed.

Sam looked in to check out. He was a bit thick-tongued from his restorative drink. He said something about "Awri' if I go now?" I half heard him. I was trying to figure out another way of trapping *him* over there into giving away the right spot. I motioned my consent absently.

He went a little unsteadily down the stairs to the ground floor and after a delaying moment or two I heard the street door close after him. Poor Sam, he wasn't much used to liquor.

I was left alone in the house, one chair the limit of my freedom of movement.

Suddenly a light went on over there again, just momentarily, to go right out again afterwards. He must have needed it for something, to locate something that he had already been looking for and found he wasn't able to put his hands on readily without it. He found it, whatever it was, almost immediately, and moved back at once to put the lights out again. As he turned to do so, I saw him give a glance out the window. He didn't come to the window to do it, he just shot it out in passing.

Something about it struck me as different from any of the others I'd seen him give in all the time I'd been watching him. If you can qualify such an elusive thing as a glance, I would have termed it a glance with a purpose. It was certainly anything but vacant or random, it had a bright spark of fixity in it. It wasn't one of those precautionary sweeps I'd seen him give, either. It hadn't started over on the other side and worked its way around to my side, the right. It had hit dead-center at my bay window, for just a split second while it lasted, and then was gone again. And the lights were gone, and he was gone.

Sometimes your senses take things in without your mind translating them into their proper meaning. My eyes saw that look. My mind refused to smelter it properly. "It was meaningless," I thought. "An unintentional bull's-eye, that just happened to hit square over here, as he went toward the lights on his way out."

Delayed action. A wordless ring of the phone. To test a voice? A period of bated darkness following that, in which two could have played at the same game—stalking one another's window-squares, unseen. A last-moment flicker of the lights, that was bad strategy but unavoidable. A parting glance, radioactive with malignant intention. All these things sank in without fusing. My eyes did their job, it was my mind that didn't—or at least took its time about it.

Seconds went by in packages of sixty. It was very still

around the familiar quadrangle formed by the back of the houses. Sort of a breathless stillness. And then a sound came into it, starting up from nowhere, nothing. The unmistakable, spaced clicking a cricket makes in the silence of the night. I thought of Sam's superstition about them, that he claimed had never failed to fulfill itself yet. If that was the case, it looked bad for somebody in one of these slumbering houses around here——

Sam had been gone only about ten minutes. And now he was back again, he must have forgotten something. That drink was responsible. Maybe his hat, or maybe even the key to his own quarters uptown. He knew I couldn't come down and let him in, and he was trying to be quiet about it, thinking perhaps I'd dozed off. All I could hear was this faint jiggling down at the lock of the front door. It was one of those old-fashioned stoop houses, with an outer pair of storm doors that were allowed to swing free all night, and then a small vestibule, and then the inner door, worked by a simple iron key. The liquor had made his hand a little unreliable, although he'd had this difficulty once or twice before, even without it. A match would have helped him find the keyhole quicker, but then, Sam doesn't smoke. I knew he wasn't likely to have one on him.

The sound had stopped now. He must have given up, gone away again, decided to let whatever it was go until tomorrow. He hadn't gotten in, because I knew his noisy way of letting doors coast shut by themselves too well, and there hadn't been any sound of that sort, that loose slap he always made.

Then suddenly it exploded. Why at this particular moment, I don't know. That was some mystery of the inner workings of my own mind. It flashed like waiting gunpowder which a spark has finally reached along a slow train. Drove all thoughts of Sam, and the front door, and this and that completely out of my head. It had been waiting there since midafternoon today, and only now—— More of that delayed action. Damn that delayed action.

The renting agent and Thorwald had both started even from the living room window. An intervening gap of blind wall, and both had reappeared at the kitchen window, still one above the other. But some sort of a hitch or flaw or jump had taken place, right there, that bothered me. The eye is a reliable surveyor. There wasn't anything the matter with their timing, it was with their parallel-ness, or whatever the word is. The hitch had been vertical, not horizontal. There had been an upward "jump."

Now I had it, now I knew. And it couldn't wait. It was too good. They wanted a body? Now I had one for them.

Sore or not, Boyne would *have* to listen to me now. I didn't waste any time, I dialed his precinct-house then and there in the dark, working the slots in my lap by memory alone. They didn't make much noise going around, just a light click. Not even as distinct as that cricket out there——

"He went home long ago," the desk sergeant said.

This couldn't wait. "All right, give me his home phone number."

He took a minute, came back again. "Trafalgar," he said. Then nothing more.

"Well? Trafalgar what?" Not a sound.

"Hello? Hello?" I tapped it. "Operator, I've been cut off. Give me that party again." I couldn't get her either.

I hadn't been cut off. My wire had been cut. That had been too sudden, right in the middle of—— And to be cut like that it would have to be done somewhere right here inside the house with me. Outside it went underground.

Delayed action. This time final, fatal, altogether too late. A voiceless ring of the phone. A direction-finder of a look from over there. "Sam" seemingly trying to get back in a while ago.

Suddenly, death was somewhere inside the house here with me. And I couldn't move, I couldn't get up out of this chair. Even if I had gotten through to Boyne just now, that would have been too late. There wasn't time enough now for one of those camera-finishes in this. I could have shouted out the window to that gallery of sleeping rear-window neighbors around me, I supposed. It would have brought them to the windows. It couldn't have brought them over here in time. By the time they had even figured which particular house it was coming from, it would stop again, be over with. I didn't open my mouth. Not because I was brave, but because it was so obviously useless.

He'd be up in a minute. He must be on the stairs now, although I couldn't hear him. Not even a creak. A creak would have been a relief, would have placed him. This was like being shut up in the dark with the silence of a gliding, coiling cobra somewhere around you.

There wasn't a weapon in the place with me. There were books there on the wall, in the dark, within reach. Me, who never read. The former owner's books. There was a bust of Rousseau or Montesquieu, I'd never been able to decide which, one of those gents with flowing manes, topping them. It was a monstrosity, bisque clay, but it too dated from before my occupancy.

I arched my middle upward from the chair seat and clawed desperately up at it. Twice my fingertips slipped off it, then at the third raking I got it to teeter, and the fourth brought it down into my lap, pushing me down into the chair. There was a steamer rug under me. I didn't need it around me in this weather, I'd been using it to soften the seat of the chair. I tugged it out from under and mantled it around me like an Indian brave's blanket. Then I squirmed far down in the chair, let my head and one shoulder dangle out over the arm, on the side next to the wall. I hoisted the bust to my other, upward shoulder, balanced it there precariously for a second head, blanket tucked around its ears. From the back, in the dark, it would look—I hoped——

I proceeded to breathe adenoidally, like someone in heavy upright sleep. It wasn't hard. My own breath was coming nearly that labored anyway, from tension.

He was good with knobs and hinges and things. I never heard the door open, and this one, unlike the one downstairs, was right behind me. A little eddy of air puffed through the dark at me. I could feel it because my scalp, the real one, was all wet at the roots of the hair right then.

If it was going to be a knife or head-blow, the dodge might give me a second chance, that was the most I could hope for, I knew. My arms and shoulders are hefty. I'd bring him down on me in a bear-hug after the first slash or drive, and break his neck or collarbone against me. If it was going to be a gun, he'd get me anyway in the end. A difference of a few seconds. He had a gun, I knew, that he was going to use on me in the open, over at Lakeside Park. I was hoping that here, indoors, in order to make his own escape more practicable——

Time was up.

The flash of the shot lit up the room for a second, it was so dark. Or at least the corners of it, like flickering, weak lightning. The bust bounced on my shoulder and disintegrated into chunks.

I thought he was jumping up and down on the floor for a minute with frustrated rage. Then when I saw him dart by me and lean over the window sill to look for a way out, the sound transferred itself rearwards and downwards, became a pummeling with hoof and hip at the street door. The camera-finish after all. But he still could have killed me five times.

I flung my body down into the narrow crevice between chair arm and wall, but my legs were still up, and so was my head and that one shoulder.

He whirled, fired at me so close that it was like looking

at sunrise in the face. I didn't feel it, so—it hadn't hit.

"You——" I heard him grunt to himself. I think it was the last thing he said. The rest of his life was all action, not verbal.

He flung over the sill on one arm and dropped into the yard. Two-story drop. He made it because he missed the cement, landed on the sod-strip in the middle. I jacked myself up over the chair arm and flung myself bodily forward at the window, neatly hitting it chin first.

He went all right. When life depends on it, you go. He took the first fence, rolled over that bellywards. He went over the second like a cat, hands and feet pointed together in a spring. Then he was back in the rear yard of his own building. He got up on something, just about like Sam had—— The rest was all footwork, with quick little corkscrew twists at each landing stage. Sam had latched his windows down when he was over there, but he'd reopened one of them for ventilation on his return. His whole life depended now on that casual, unthinking little act——

Second, third. He was up to his own windows. He'd made it. Something went wrong. He veered out away from them in another pretzel-twist, flashed up toward the fifth, the one above. Something sparked in the darkness of one of his own windows where he'd been just now, and a shot thudded heavily out around the quadrangle-enclosure like a big bass drum.

He passed the fifth, the sixth, got to the roof. He'd made it a second time. Gee, he loved life! The guys in his own windows couldn't get him, he was over them in a straight line and there was too much fire escape interlacing in the way.

I was too busy watching him to watch what was going on around me. Suddenly Boyne was next to me, sighting. I heard him mutter: "I almost hate to do this, he's got to fall so far."

He was balanced on the roof parapet up there, with a

star right over his head. An unlucky star. He stayed a
minute too long, trying to kill before he was killed. Or
maybe he was killed, and knew it.

A shot cracked, high up against the sky, the window
pane flew apart all over the two of us, and one of the
books snapped right behind me.

Boyne didn't say anything more about hating to do it.
My face was pressing outward against his arm. The
recoil of his elbow jarred my teeth. I blew a clearing
through the smoke to watch him go.

It was pretty horrible. He took a minute to show anything, standing up there on the parapet. Then he let his
gun go, as if to say: "I won't need this any more." Then
he went after it. He missed the fire escape entirely, came
all the way down on the outside. He landed so far out he
hit one of the projecting planks, down there out of sight.
It bounced his body up, like a springboard. Then it
landed again—for good. And that was all.

I said to Boyne: "I got it. I got it finally. The fifth-floor
flat, the one over his, that they're still working on. The
cement kitchen floor, raised above the level of the other
rooms. They wanted to comply with the fire laws and
also obtain a dropped living room effect, as cheaply as
possible. Dig it up——"

He went right over then and there, down through the
basement and over the fences, to save time. The electricity wasn't turned on yet in that one, they had to use their
torches. It didn't take them long at that, once they'd got
started. In about half an hour he came to the window
and wigwagged over for my benefit. It meant yes.

He didn't come over until nearly eight in the morning;
after they'd tidied up and taken them away. Both away,
the hot dead and the cold dead. He said: "Jeff, I take it
all back. That damn fool that I sent up there about the
trunk—well, it wasn't his fault, in a way. I'm to blame.
He didn't have orders to check on the woman's descrip-
tion, only on the contents of the trunk. He came back

and touched on it in a general way. I go home and I'm in bed already, and suddenly pop! into my brain—one of the tenants I questioned two whole days ago had given us a few details and they didn't tally with his on several important points. Talk about being slow to catch on!"

"I've had that all the way through this damn thing," I admitted ruefully. "I called it delayed action. It nearly killed me."

"I'm a police officer and you're not."

"That how you happened to shine at the right time?"

"Sure. We came over to pick him up for questioning. I left them planted there when we saw he wasn't in, and came on over here by myself to square it up with you while we were waiting. How did you happen to hit on that cement floor?"

I told him about the freak synchronization. "The renting agent showed up taller at the kitchen window in proportion to Thorwald, than he had been a moment before when both were at the living room windows together. It was no secret that they were putting in cement floors, topped by a cork composition, and raising them considerably. But it took on new meaning. Since the top floor one has been finished for some time, it had to be the fifth. Here's the way I have it lined up, just in theory. She's been in ill health for years, and he's been out of work, and he got sick of that and of her both. Met this other——"

"She'll be here later today, they're bringing her down under arrest."

"He probably insured her for all he could get, and then started to poison her slowly, trying not to leave any trace. I imagine—and remember, this is pure conjecture —she caught him at it that night the light was on all night. Caught on in some way, or caught him in the act. He lost his head, and did the very thing he had wanted all along to avoid doing. Killed her by violence— strangulation or a blow. The rest had to be hastily im-

provised. He got a better break than he deserved at
that. He thought of the apartment upstairs, went up and
looked around. They'd just finished laying the floor, the
cement hadn't hardened yet, and the materials were still
around. He gouged a trough out of it just wide enough to
take her body, put her in it, mixed fresh cement and
recemented over her, possibly raising the general level of
the floor an inch or two so that she'd be safely covered. A
permanent, odorless coffin. Next day the workmen came
back, laid down the cork surfacing on top of it without
noticing anything, I suppose he'd used one of their own
trowels to smooth it. Then he sent his accessory upstate
fast, near where his wife had been several summers
before, but to a different farmhouse where she wouldn't
be recognized, along with the trunk keys. Sent the trunk
up after her, and dropped himself an already used post
card into his mailbox, with the year-date blurred. In a
week or two she would have probably committed 'sui-
cide' up there as Mrs. Anna Thorwald. Despondency
due to ill health. Written him a farewell note and left her
clothes beside some body of deep water. It was risky, but
they might have succeeded in collecting the insurance at
that."

By nine Boyne and the rest had gone. I was still sitting
there in the chair, too keyed up to sleep. Sam came in
and said: "Here's Doc Preston."

He showed up rubbing his hands, in that way he has.
"Guess we can take that cast off your leg now. You must
be tired of sitting there all day doing nothing."

POST-MORTEM

THE WOMAN WONDERED WHO they were and
what they wanted out there at this time of the day. She
knew they couldn't be salesmen, because salesmen don't
travel around in threes. She put down her mop, wiped
her hands nervously on her apron, started for the door.

What could be wrong? Nothing had happened to Stephen, had it? She was trembling with agitation and her
face was pale under its light golden tan by the time she
had opened the door and stood confronting them. They
all had white cards stuck in their hat bands, she noticed.

They crowded eagerly forward, each one trying to
edge the others aside. "Mrs. Mead?" the foremost one
said.

"Wha-what is it?" she quavered.

"Have you been listening to your radio?"

"No, one of the tubes burned out."

She saw them exchange zestful glances. "She hasn't
heard yet!" Their spokesman went on: "We've got good
news for you!"

She was still as frightened as ever. "Good news?" she
repeated timidly.

"Yes. Can't you guess?"

"N-no."

They kept prolonging the suspense unendurably. "You
know what day this is, don't you?"

She shook her head. She was wishing they'd go away,
but she didn't have the sharp-tongued facility of some

housewives for ridding themselves of unwelcome intruders.

"It's the day the Derby is run off!" They waited expectantly. Her face didn't show any enlightenment whatever. "Can't you guess why we're here, Mrs. Mead? *Your horse has come in first!*"

She still showed only bewilderment. Disappointment was acutely visible on all their faces. "My horse?" she said blankly. "I don't own any hor—"

"No, no, no, Mrs. Mead, don't you understand? We're newspaper men; word has just flashed to our offices from London that you're one of the three Americans to hold a ticket on Ravenal in the sweepstakes. The other two are in 'Frisco and in Boston."

They had forced her half-way down the short front hall by now, back toward the kitchen, simply by crowding in on her. "Don't you understand what we're trying to tell you? It means you've won a hundred and fifty thousand dollars!"

Luckily there happened to be a chair at hand, up against the wall. She dropped down on it limply. "Oh, no!"

They eyed her in baffled surprise. She wasn't taking this at all the way they'd expected. She kept shaking her head, mildly but obstinately. "No, gentlemen. There must be some mistake somewhere. It must be somebody else by the same name. You see, I haven't any ticket on Rav— What'd you say that horse's name was? I haven't any sweepstakes ticket at all."

The four of them regarded her reproachfully, as though they felt she was trying to put one over on them.

"Sure you have, you must have. Where'd they get your name and address from, otherwise? It was cabled to our offices from London, along with the names of the other winners. They didn't just make it up out of thin air. It must have been down on the slip that was dug up out of the drum in Dublin before the race. What're you trying to do, kid us, Mrs. Mead?"

She perked up her head alertly at that, as though something had occurred to her just then for the first time.

"Just a moment, I never stopped to think! You keep calling me Mead. Mead is no longer my name, since I remarried. My present name is Mrs. Archer. But I've been so used to hearing Mead for years, and the sight of so many of you at the door all at one time flustered me so, that I never noticed you were using it until now.

"If this winning ticket is in the name of Mrs. Mead, as you say, then Harry, my first husband, must have bought it in my name shortly before his death, and never told me about it. Yes, that must be it, particularly if this address was given in the cable report. You see, the house was in my name, and I stayed on here after I lost Harry, and even after my remarriage." She looked up at them help-lessly. "But where is it, the counterfoil or whatever they call it? I haven't the faintest idea."

They stared in dismay. "You mean you don't know where it is, Mrs. Mea— Mrs. Archer?"

"I never even knew he'd bought one, until now. He never said a word to me about it. He may have wanted to surprise me, in case it won something." She gazed sadly down at the floor. "Poor dear, he died quite suddenly," she said softly.

Their consternation far surpassed her own. It was almost comical; you would have thought the money came out of their pockets instead of hers. They all began talking at once, showering questions and suggestions on her.

"Gee, you'd better look around good and see if you can't find it! You can't collect the money without it, you know, Mrs. Archer."

"Have you gotten rid of all his effects yet? It may still be among them."

"Did he have a desk where he kept old papers? Should we help you look, Mrs. Archer?"

The telephone began to ring. The poor woman put her hands distractedly to her head, lost a little of her equanimity, which wasn't to be wondered at. "Please go now, all of you," she urged impatiently. "You're upsetting me so that I really can't think straight!"

They went out jabbering about it among themselves. "This makes a better human-interest story than if she had it! I'm going to write it up this way."

Mrs. Archer was answering the phone by now. "Yes, Stephen, some reporters who were here just now told me about it. It must still be around some place; a thing like that wouldn't just *disappear*, would it? Good; I wish you would."

He'd said, "A hundred and fifty thousand dollars is too much money to let slip through our fingers that easily." He'd said, "I'm coming home to help you look for it."

Forty-eight hours later they'd reached the end of their ingenuity. Or rather, forty-eight hours later they finally were willing to admit defeat. They'd actually reached the end of their ingenuity long before then.

"Crying won't help any!" Stephen Archer remarked testily across the table to her. Their nerves were on edge, anyone's would have been by this time, so she didn't resent the sharpness of his tone.

She smothered a sob, dabbed at her eyes. "I know, but—it's agonizing. So near and yet so far! Coming into all that money would have been a turning point in both our lives. It would have been the difference between living and merely existing. All the things we've wanted so, done without. . . . And to have to sit helplessly by and watch it dance away like a will o' the wisp! I almost wish they'd never come here and told me about it."

The table between them was littered with scrawled-over scraps of paper. On them was a curious sort of inventory. An inventory of the belongings of the late Harry Mead. One list was headed: "Bags, suitcases, etc." Another: "Desk, office desk, drawers, etc." A third: "Suits." And so on. Most of these things were hopelessly scattered and lost track of by now, a few were still in their possession. They had wanted to reconstruct his entire accumulation of physical properties, as it stood at or just before his death, in order to trace the ticket through all possible channels of disappearance. A hopeless task.

Some were checked. Others had question marks beside them. Still others had crosses after them, marking their elimination as possibilities. Stephen Archer had been methodical about it to say the least; anyone would have been, for one hundred and fifty thousand dollars.

They'd gone over them item by item, ten, twenty, fifty times, adding, discarding, revising, as the physical search kept pace with the inventory. Slowly the checks and crosses had overtaken and outnumbered the question marks. They'd even got in touch with people, former friends, business acquaintances of the dead man, his barber, his favorite bartender, the youth who had shined his shoes once a week, as many of them as they could think of and reach, to find out if maybe casually one day he hadn't mentioned buying such a ticket, and more to the point, happened to mention where he'd put it. He hadn't. If he hadn't thought it important enough to mention to his own wife, why would he mention it to an outsider?

Archer broke off tapping his nails on the table edge, shoved his chair back exasperatedly, squeezed his eyelids. "It's driving me nuts! I'm going out for a walk. Maybe something'll come to me while I'm by myself." He picked up his hat, called back from the front door: "*Try*, will you, Josie? Keep trying!" That was all he'd been saying for the past two days and they were still no further. "And don't let anyone in while I'm gone," he added. That was another thing. They'd been pestered to within an inch of their lives, as might have been expected. Reporters, strangers, curiosity mongers.

He'd hardly turned off at the end of the front walk than the doorbell rang. In fact it was such a short time after, that she was sure it was he, come back for his latchkey, or to tell her some new possibility that had just occurred to him. Every time he'd left the house the last two days he'd come back again two or three times to tell her some new idea that had just struck him—of where it could be. But none of them were ever any good.

But when she opened it she saw her mistake: it was one of those three reporters from the other day. Alone, this time.

"Any luck yet, Mrs. Archer? I saw your husband just leaving the house, so I thought I'd find out from you. He's been hanging up the phone every time I tried to call."

"No, we haven't found it. And he told me not to talk to anyone."

"I know, but why don't you let me see if I can help you? I'm not here as a reporter now; my paper ran the story long ago. It's the human angle of the thing has got me. I'd like to do what I can to help you."

"How can you?" she said doubtfully. "We've gotten nowhere ourselves, so how could an outsider possibly succeed?"

"Three heads are better than two."

She stood aside reluctantly, let him pass. "You'll have to go before he comes back, I know he won't like it if he finds you here. But I *would* like to talk it over with someone; we are at our wits' end."

He took off his hat as he came in. "Thank you, Mrs. Archer. My name's Westcott."

They sat down on opposite sides of the paper-littered round table, he in the same chair Archer had been in before. She crossed her wrists dejectedly on the table top. "Well, we've tried everything," she said helplessly. "What can you suggest?"

"He didn't sell it, because a thing like that is not transferable; your name was down on the stub that went to Dublin, and you would still remain the payee. He may possibly have lost it, though."

She shook her head firmly. "My husband suggested that too, but I know better. Not Harry; he never lost a pin in his whole lifetime! Besides if he had, I know he would have told me about it, even if he didn't tell me about buying it in the first place. He was a thrifty type of man; it would have upset him too much to lose two-and-a-half dollars' worth of anything to be able to keep still about it."

"Then we're safe in saying he still had it when he died. But *where*, that's the thing. Because wherever it was *then*, it still is *now*, most likely."

He was riffling through the scraps of paper while he spoke, reading the headings to himself. "What about wallets or billfolds? I don't see any list of them."

"He didn't have one to his name, never used them. He was the sort who preferred to carry things loose in his pockets. I remember I tried to give him one once, and he exchanged it right after the holidays."

"How about books? People use funny things for bookmarks, sometimes, and then the objects stay in between the pages and have a habit of getting lost."

"We've covered that. Harry and I were never great readers, we didn't belong to any public or circulating libraries, so the one or two books that were in the house didn't leave it again afterwards. And the same one or two that were here in Harry's day are still here now. I've turned them upside-down, shaken them out thoroughly, examined them page by page."

He picked up another slip. "He only owned three suits?"

"It was hard to get him to buy a new one; he wasn't much given to dress."

"Did you dispose of them after he died?"

"Only one of them, the brown. The gray is still up there in the storeroom. It was so old and threadbare I was ashamed to even show it to the old clothes dealer who took the other one, to tell the truth. Harry had lived in it for years; I wouldn't let him be seen out in it, toward the end. He just used it around the house."

"Well, what about the one you did give away, or sell? Did you go through the pockets before you disposed of it? It may have remained in one of them."

"No, I'm absolutely sure it didn't. The woman never lived, Mr. Westcott, I don't care who she is, who didn't probe through pockets, turn the linings inside out, before she got rid of any of her husband's old clothes. It's as much an instinctive feminine gesture as primping the hair. I recall distinctly doing that—it wasn't very long ago, after all—and there was nothing in those pockets."

"I see." He stroked his chin reflectively. "And what about this third one you have down—dark blue double-breasted? What became of that?"

She lowered her eyes deprecatingly. "That was practically brand new; he'd only worn it once before he died. Well, when he died, money wasn't any too plentiful, so instead of buying a new outfit, I gave it to them and had them . . . put him in it."

"He was buried in it, in other words."

"Yes. It wouldn't be in that, naturally."

He looked at her a minute before answering. Finally he said, "Why not?" Before she could answer that, except by a startled look, he went on: "Well, do you mind if we talk about it for a minute, anyway."

"No, but what——"

"Would you have approved of his buying a thing like this sweepstakes ticket, if you had known about it at the time?"

"No," she admitted. "I used to scold him about things like that, buying chances on Thanksgiving turkeys and drawing numbers out of punch boards. I considered it money thrown out. He went ahead doing it, though."

"He wouldn't want you to know he had this ticket then—unless it paid off—as, in fact, it did. So he'd put it in the place you were least likely to come upon it. That's logical, isn't it?"

"I suppose so."

"Another question: I suppose you brushed off his clothes from time to time, the way most wives do, especially when he had so few suits?"

"Yes, the brown, the one he wore daily to work."

"Not the dark blue?"

"It was new, he'd only had it on his back once, there was no need to yet."

"He probably knew that. He'd also know, therefore, that the safest place for him to put a sweepstakes ticket—in case he didn't want you to come across it in the course of one of your daily brushings—would be in one of the pockets of that unworn dark blue suit."

Her face was starting to pale dreadfully.

He looked at her solemnly. "I think we've found that elusive counterfoil at last. I'm very much afraid it's still with your late husband."

She stared at him with a mixture of dawning hope and horror. Dawning hope that the exhausting mystery was at last solved. Horror at what was implied if the solution were to be carried through to its logical conclusion. "What can I do about it?" she breathed fearfully.

"There's only one thing you can do. Get a permit to exhume the coffin."

She shuddered. "How can I contemplate such a thing? Suppose we're mistaken?"

"I'm sure we're not, or I wouldn't suggest your doing it."

And he could tell by looking at her that she was sure too, by now. Her objections died lingeringly, but they died one by one. "But wouldn't they, the men who prepared him, have found it themselves just before they put the suit on him, and returned it to me, if it was in that suit?"

"In the case of anything bulky, such as a thick envelope or a notebook, they probably would have. But a tissue-thin ticket like that, you know how flimsy they are, could easily have been overlooked, in the depths of one of the vest pockets, for instance."

She was growing used to the idea, repellent as it had seemed at first glance. "I really think that's what must have happened, and I want to thank you for helping us out. I'll talk it over with Mr. Archer when he comes back, hear what he says."

Westcott cleared his throat deprecatingly as he moved toward the front door. "Maybe you'd better let him think the idea was your own, not mention me at all. He might consider it butting in on the part of an outsider, and resent it. You know how it is. I'll drop by tomorrow and you can let me know what you've decided to do about it. You see, if you go ahead with the disinterment, I'd like an exclusive on it for my paper." He touched the press card stuck in his hat band, on which was written *"Bulletin."*

"I'll see that you get one," she promised him. "Good night."

When Archer had returned from his walk, she let him hang up his hat and slump frustratedly back into the chair he'd been in earlier, before coming out with it.

"Stephen, I know where it is now!" she blurted out with positive assurance.

He stopped raking fingers through his hair, jerked his

face toward her. "You sure this time, or is it just another false alarm?"

"No, this time I'm sure!" Without mentioning Westcott or his visit, she rapidly outlined his theory and also the steps by which he had built it up. "So I'm certain it's in the—casket with him. The one and only time he wore that suit before his death was one Sunday afternoon when he went out for a stroll and stopped in at a taproom for a couple of beers. What more likely place than that for him to have bought it? And then he simply left it in the suit, knowing I wouldn't be apt to find it."

She had expected him to be overjoyed, not even to feel her own preliminary qualms—which she'd overcome by now anyway. It wasn't that her line of reasoning hadn't convinced him. She could see at a glance that it had, by the way his face first lit up; but then it grew strangely pale immediately afterwards.

"We can kiss it good-bye, then!" he said huskily.

"But why, Stephen? All we need to do is to get permission to——"

There was no mistaking his pallor. He was ashen with some emotion or other. She took it to be repugnance. "I won't stand for it! If it's there, it'll have to stay there!"

"But, Stephen, I don't understand. Harry really meant nothing to you, why should you feel that way about it? If I don't object, why should you?"

"Because it's—it's like sacrilege! It gives me the creeps! If we've got to disturb the dead to come into that money, I'd rather let it go." He was on his feet now, one clenched fist on the table-top. The wrist that stemmed from it was visibly tremulous. "Anyway, I'm superstitious; I say no good can come of it."

"But that's the one thing you're not, Stephen," she contradicted gently but firmly. "You've always made a point of walking under ladders every time you see one, simply to prove you aren't superstitious. Now you say you are!"

Instead of calming him, her persistence seemed to have an adverse effect, nearly drove him frantic. His voice shook. "As your husband, I forbid you to disturb that man's remains!"

She gazed at him uncomprehendingly. "But why are you so jumpy about it? Why is your face so white? I never saw you like this before."

He wrenched at his collar as though it were choking him. "Shut up about it! Forget there ever was such a sweepstakes ticket! Forget all about the hundred and fifty thousand!" And he poured himself a double drink, but he only got half of it in the glass, his hand trembled so.

Little Mrs. Archer followed Westcott out of the taxi with a visible effort. Despite her tan, her face was deathly white under the bleaching scrutiny of the arc lights at the cemetery entrance. A night watchman, advised beforehand of their arrival and its purpose, opened a small pedestrian wicket for them in the massive grilled gates, closed since sunset.

"Don't take it that way," the newspaper man tried to reassure her. "We're not guilty of any crime by coming here and doing this. We have a court order all properly signed and perfectly legal. Your consent is all that's necessary, and you signed the application. Archer's isn't. You're the deceased's wife; he's no kin to him."

"I know, but when he finds out . . ." She cast a look behind her into the surrounding dark, almost as though fearful Archer had followed them out here. "I wonder why he was so opposed——"

Westcott gave her a look as much as to say, "So do I," but didn't answer.

"Will it take very long?" she quavered as they followed the watchman toward a little gatekeeper's lodge just within the entrance.

"They've been at work already for half an hour. I

phoned ahead as soon as the permit was okayed, to save time. They ought to be about ready for us by now."

She stiffened spasmodically against his arm, which was linked protectively to hers. "You won't have to look," he calmed her. "I know it makes it seem twice as bad, to come here at night like this, after the place is already closed for the day, but I figured this way we could do it without attracting a lot of annoying publicity and attention. Just look at it this way: With part of the money you can build him a classy mausoleum if you want to, to make up for it. Now just sit here in this little cubbyhole and try to keep your mind off it. I'll be back just as soon as—it's been done."

She gave him a wan smile under the dim electric light of the gatekeeper's lodge. "Make sure he's—it's put back properly afterwards." She was trying to be brave about it, but then it would have been a trying experience for any woman.

Westcott followed the watchman along the main graveled walk that seemed to bisect the place, the white pill of his guide's torch rolling along the ground in front of them. They turned aside at a particular little lane, and trod Indian-file until they had come to a group of motionless figures eerily waiting for them by the light of a couple of lanterns placed on the ground.

The plot had been converted into an open trough now, hillocks of displaced fill ringing it around. A withered wreath that had topped it had been cast aside. Mead had died too recently for any headstone or marker to be erected yet.

The casket was up and straddling the hillock of excavated soil, waiting for Westcott to get there. The workmen were resting on their shovels, perfectly unconcerned.

"All right, go ahead," Westcott said curtly. "Here's the authorization."

They took a cold chisel to the lid, hammered it in for a

wedge along the seam in various places, sprang the lid. Then they pried it with a crowbar. Just the way any crate or packing case is opened. The squealing and grating of the distorted nails was ghastly, though. Westcott kept taking short turns to and fro in the background while it was going on. He was glad now that he'd had sense enough to leave Mrs. Archer at the entrance to the grounds. It was no place for a woman.

Finally the sounds stopped and he knew they were ready for him. One of the workmen said with unintentional callousness: "It's all yours, mister."

Westcott threw his cigarette away, with a grimace as though it had tasted bad. He went over and squatted on his haunches beside the open coffin. Somebody was helpfully keeping the pill of white trained directly down before him. "Can you see?"

Westcott involuntarily turned his head aside, then turned it back again. "More than I care to. Keep it off the face, will you? I just want something in the pockets."

It fluctuated accommodatingly, giving an eery impression of motion to the contents of the coffin. The watchman silently handed him a pair of rubber gloves over his shoulder. Westcott drew them on with a faint snapping sound, audible in the intense stillness that hung over the little group.

It didn't take long. He reached down and unbuttoned the double-breasted jacket, laid it open. The men around him drew back a step. His hand went unhesitatingly toward the upper-left vest-pocket. If it required mental effort to make it do so, it wasn't visible. Two fingers hooked searchingly, disappeared into blue serge. They came out again empty, shifted to the lower pocket on that same side, sheathed themselves again. They came up with a folded square of crepe-like paper, that rattled like a dry leaf.

"Got it," Westcott remarked tonelessly.

The men ringing him around, or at least the one wielding the torch, must have been over to peer at it. The pill of light shifted inadvertently upward again. Westcott blinked. "Keep it away from the face. I told——" It obediently corrected itself. He must have given a double-take-'em in the brief instant it had been up where it shouldn't. "Put it on the face!" he suddenly countermanded.

The sweepstakes ticket, the center of attraction until now, fell back on the vest, lay there unnoticed. Westcott only had eyes for that white light on the face. An abnormal silence hung suspended over the macabre scene. It was like a still-life, they were all so motionless.

Westcott broke it at last. He only said two things. "Um-hum," with a corroborative shake of his head. And then, "Autopsy." He said the latter after he'd finally straightened to his feet and retrieved the discarded ticket as an afterthought. . . .

Mrs. Archer was still standing beside him in the caretaker's lodge, salvaged ticket clutched in her hand, when men, carrying the coffin, went by in the gloom a few minutes later. The lantern leading the way revealed it to her.

She clutched at his sleeve. "What's that they're carrying out? That isn't *it*, is it? What's that closed car, like a small delivery truck, that just drove up outside the grounds?"

"That's from the morgue, Mrs. Archer."

"But why? What's happened?" For the second time that night the ticket fluttered, discarded, to the ground.

"Nothing, Mrs. Archer. Let's go now, shall we? I want to have a talk with you before you go home."

As she was about to re-enter the taxi they had kept waiting for them outside the grounds, she drew back. "Just a minute. I promised Stephen to bring an evening paper back with me when I came home. There's a newsstand over there on the other side of the roadway."

Westcott waited by the cab while she went over to it

alone. It occurred to her it would be a good idea to see
whether or not he had written up anything beforehand
about the missing ticket's whereabouts. If it wasn't
already too late, she wanted to prevail upon him not to,
if possible. "Let me have the *Bulletin*, please."

The news vendor shook his head. "Never heard of it,
lady. No such paper in this town."

"Are you sure?" she cried thunderstruck. She glanced
across the street to the figure waiting for her by the taxi.

"I oughta be, lady. I handle every paper published in
the city and I never yet come across one called the
Bulletin!"

When she rejoined Westcott, she explained quietly, "I
changed my mind." She glanced up at the press card
sticking in his hat band. "*Bulletin*" was plainly to be
seen, typed on it.

She was very quiet in the taxi riding homeward,
seemed lost in thought. The only sign she gave was an
occasional gnawing at the lining of her cheek.

"I've been assigned to do a feature article about you,
Mrs. Archer," Westcott began when they were seated in
the little cafeteria to which he had brought her. "Human-
interest stuff, you know. That's why I'd like to ask you a
few questions."

She looked at him without answering. She was still
gnawing the lining of her cheek, lost in thought.

"Mead died quite suddenly, didn't he? Just what were
the circumstances?"

"He hadn't been feeling well for several days . . . indigestion. We'd finished dinner that night and I was doing
the dishes. He complained of feeling ill and I suggested
he go outside the house for a breath of fresh air. He went
out in back, to putter around in the little truck-garden he
was trying to raise."

"In the dark?"

"He took a pocket-light with him."

"Go ahead." He was taking notes in shorthand or

something while she spoke—as newspapermen *don't* do.

"About half an hour went by. One time I heard a crash somewhere near at hand, but nothing else, so I didn't investigate. Then shortly after, Stephen—Mr. Archer—dropped around for a friendly visit. He'd been doing that those last few weeks; he and Harry would sit and chew the rag the way men do, over a couple of highballs.

"Well, I went to the back door to call Harry in. I could see his light lying out there on the ground, but he didn't answer. We found him lying there, writhing and unable to speak. His eyes were rolling and he seemed to be in convulsions. Stephen and I carried him in between us and I phoned for the doctor, but by the time he'd come, Harry was already dead. The doctor told us it was an attack of acute indigestion, plus a shock to his heart, perhaps brought on by the noise of that crash I told you about."

He lidded his eyes at her. "I am convinced that 'crash' had something to do with bringing it on. And you mean the coroner passed it off as acute indigestion, went on record in his official report to that effect? That's something for the municipal council to take up later."

"Why?" she gasped.

He went ahead as though he hadn't heard her. "You say Archer was the salesman who insured Mead? In your favor, of course?"

"Yes."

"Was it for a large amount?"

"Is it necessary to know all this for a newspaper article? You're no reporter, Mr. Westcott, and never were; there's no such paper as the *Bulletin*. You're a detective." Her voice frayed with hysteria. "What are you questioning me like this for?"

He said, "I'll answer that when I come back. Will you excuse me a minute, I want to make a phone call. Stay right where you are, Mrs. Archer."

He kept his eye on her while he was standing beside

the wall phone across the room, dialing, and then asking a brief question or two. She sat there in a state of dazed apprehension, occasionally moistening her lips with the tip of her tongue.

She repeated her question when he had seated himself again. "What do you want with me? Why are you questioning me about Harry's death?"

"Because I found the skin was broken as if from a blow on your first husband's skull when I had the remains disinterred earlier tonight. I phoned the morgue; they've just made a hasty examination and told me the skull was fractured!"

Her face paled to an unearthly gray. He hadn't realized until now that she was lightly tanned to an even, golden hue like a biscuit all over her face, neck and arms. Her paling beneath it revealed it. She had to grip the table edge with both hands. For a minute he thought she was going to topple over, chair and all. He spaded a hand out toward her to support her, but it wasn't necessary. He handed her a glass of water. She barely touched her lips to it, then took a deep breath.

"Then that was Harry's coffin that I saw them carry past us in the dark, out there?"

He nodded, riffled the scraps of paper he had been taking notes on. "Now let me get the story straight." But his eyes were boring into her tormented face like gimlets instead of consulting the "notes" while he spoke.

"Stephen Archer insured your first husband's life heavily, in your favor. He became his friend, fell into the habit of dropping over to the house of an evening and sitting and chatting with him.

"The night of his death Mead went out into the dark behind the house. You heard a sound like a crash. Then Archer came to the front door of the house not long after. When you went to call your husband, he was dying, and he died. A private physician and the municipal coroner both passed it off as acute indigestion. Both those gent's finances and ethics are going to be investigated—but I'm not concerned with that now, I'm only concerned with the part up to your husband's death. That's my job. Now, have I got the story straight?"

She took so long to answer that it almost seemed as if she wasn't going to, but still he waited. And finally she did. With the impassive, frozen face of a woman who has made a momentous decision and put all thought of the consequences behind her.

"No," she said, "you haven't got it straight. Shall we go over it a second time? First, would you mind tearing up those notes you made? They will have very little bearing on it by the time I'm through."

He tore them up into small pieces and dribbled them onto the floor, smiling as though he had intended doing that all along. "Now, Mrs. Archer."

She spoke like a person in their sleep, eyes centered high over his head, as if drawing her inspiration from the ceiling. "Stephen attracted me from the first time I saw him. He was not to blame in any way for what happened. He came over to see Harry, not me. But the more I saw him, the stronger the feeling grew on my part. Harry was heavily insured in my favor. I couldn't help thinking how opportune it would be if—anything took him from me. I would be comfortably well off, and since Stephen was unmarried, what was to prevent my eventual remarriage to him? From thinking it became day-dreaming, from day-dreaming it became action.

"That night when Harry went out in back of the house to get some air, I thought it out for the last time, while doing the dishes. Suddenly I found myself carrying it out. I went upstairs, got out an—an old flat-iron I no longer used. I came downstairs with it, hidden under my kitchen apron, and, in the dark, went out to him. I knew Stephen was coming over later, that was all I could think of. Harry was no longer my husband, someone I loved; to me he had become just an obstacle standing between Stephen and myself.

"I stood and chatted with him a moment, wondering how I was going to do it. I wasn't afraid of being heard or seen, our house stands by itself, 'way out. But I was afraid of the look there would be in his eyes at the last moment. Suddenly I saw a firefly behind him. I said, 'Look, dear, there's a firefly, in your radishes.'

"He turned his back to me, and I did it. I swung the flat-iron by its handle, squarely at the back of his head. He didn't die right away, but his brain was already paralyzed and he couldn't talk, so I saw it was all over. I went further out into the fields and buried the iron, using his garden hoe.

"Then I returned to the house, washed up. Just as I got through, Stephen came around. I went out to the back door with him, pretended to call Harry. Then we found him and carried him in. Stephen has never found out to this day that I did it."

"You mean he didn't notice the wound? Didn't it bleed?"

"It did a little, but I had washed it off. I took some pinkish face enamel that I used on myself to hide wrinkles, plastered the wound over with that, and even powdered it so that it would be less noticeable. He was slightly bald, you know. And I combed his hair to conceal it completely. I made a good job of it, after all I've been using the enamel stuff for years."

"Very interesting. And it evidently passed muster with the doctor you called, the coroner, and finally the undertaker who prepared him. That explains that. Now, did you hit him squarely in the back of the head—or a little to one side, say the left."

She paused. Then: "Yes, a little to the left."

"You can show me where it is you buried the weapon afterwards, I suppose?"

"No, I—I dug it up again afterwards, and then one time when I was crossing the river on the ferry to visit my sister-in-law, I dropped it in, out in the middle."

"But you *can* tell me how much it weighed? Was it large or——"

She shook her head. "I know I'm very stupid, but I couldn't say. Just a flat-iron."

"After you'd had it all those years?" He sighed ruefully. "But at least it *was* a flat-iron, you're sure of that?"

"Oh, yes."

"Well, that about covers everything." He stood up. "I know you're tired, and I won't keep you any longer. Thanks a lot, and good night, Mrs. Archer."

"Good night?" she echoed nonplused. "You mean you're not going to hold me, not going to arrest me, after what I've just told you?"

"Much as I'd like to accommodate you," he said drily, "there are one or two little loose threads; oh, nothing much to speak of, but just enough to impede a nice clean-cut arrest, such as you seem to have your loyal wifely heart set on. Taking them at random, there isn't a wrinkle on your entire face, so it shows a lot of mistaken diligence on your part if you actually do use any pinkish facial enamel as you say.

"And secondly, he wasn't hit on the back of the head, but high on the right temple. You wouldn't forget a thing like that! And there was no hair on his temple, Mrs. Archer."

Suddenly she crumpled, buried her face in her arms on the table. "Oh, I know what you're going to think now! Stephen didn't do it, I know he didn't! You're not going to——"

"I'm not going to do anything for the present. But on one condition only: I want your solemn promise not to mention this conversation to him. Nor about my having the remains sent down to the morgue, nor any of the rest of it. Otherwise, I'll arrest him as a precautionary measure and have him held. And he'll have a hard time getting out of it, even if not guilty."

She was almost abject in her gratitude. "Oh, I promise, I promise! I swear I won't say a word! But I'm sure you'll find out that he didn't! He's so kind and considerate of me, so thoughtful."

"You, in turn, are insured in his favor, I suppose?"

"Oh, yes, but there's nothing in that. Somebody has to be beneficiary, and I have no children nor close relatives. You're entirely mistaken if you suspect him of harboring such thoughts! Why, if I even catch the slightest cold, he's as worried as he can be! A week or so ago I had a slight chest cold, and he rushed me right to the doctor, all upset about it. He even brought home one of these sun lamps, has insisted on my taking treatments with it ever since, to build up my resistance. Of course it's sort of a nuisance to have around the place but——"

He was leading her outside while she jabbered, looking around and trying to find a taxi to send her off in. The conversation no longer seemed to hold much interest for him. "That so? In what way?"

"Well, the bathroom's tiny to begin with, and it's constantly falling over on top of me. He insists the best time to use it is while I'm in the tub, in that way I'm entirely uncovered and can get the best results."

He was still looking around for a taxi to get her off his hands. "They're rather heavy, aren't they?"

"No, long and spindly. But luckily he's been there each time, to right it again."

"*Each* time?" was all he said.

"Yes." She laughed deprecatingly, as if trying to build up a disarming picture of her devoted husband for him, turn this man's suspicions away from anyone so good-hearted and generous. "I always wait until after he's left the house in the mornings to take my bath. But then he almost always forgets something at the last minute after he's already at the station, and comes dashing back and blundering into the bathroom, and over it goes."

"What sort of things does he forget?" He'd found her a taxi, but now he was keeping it waiting.

"Oh, one day a clean handkerchief; the next certain papers, that he needs; the next, his fountain pen——"

"But does he keep those things in the bathroom?"

She laughed again. "No. But he never can find where they are, so he comes barging into the bathroom to ask me—and then over goes the lamp!"

"And this happens practically every time you have it turned on?"

"I don't think it's missed once."

It was now he who was looking up over her head, just as she had before. The last thing he said, as he took leave of her, was: "You'll keep your promise not to mention this interview to your husband?"

"I will," she assured him.

"Oh, and one other thing. Postpone your bath and sun lamp treatment for just a few minutes tomorrow morning. I may want to question you further, as soon as your husband leaves the house, and I wouldn't want to get you out of the tub once you're in it."

Stephen Archer shot up from his chair when she entered, as though a spring had been released under him. She couldn't identify the emotion that gripped him, save that whatever it was, it was strong. Some sort of anxiety. "You must have sat through the show twice!" he accused her.

"Stephen, I——" She fumbled in her purse. "I didn't go to a picture. I got it!" Suddenly it lay on the table between them. Just as it had come out of the vest pocket. "I did what you told me not to."

The way his eyes dilated she thought they would shoot out of his face. Suddenly he had her by the shoulders, gripping her like a vise. "Who was with you? Who saw it—done?"

"Nobody. I obtained a permit, and I took it out there and showed it to the man in charge of the grounds, and he got a couple of workmen——" Westcott's warning was in her mind, like a cautioning finger.

"Yes. Go on." His grip never relaxed.

"One of them got it out of the vest pocket, and then they put the lid on again and lowered it, and covered it up."

Breath slowly hissed from his knotted lips as from a safety valve. His hands left her shoulders.

"Look, Stephen—$150,000! Here, on the table before us! Wouldn't anyone have done the same thing, if they had to?"

He didn't seem interested in the ticket. His eyes kept boring into hers. "And you're sure it was put back again, just the way it was?"

She didn't say a word more.

He felt for the back of his neck. "I'd hate to think—he wasn't left just the way he was," he said lamely. He left her there and went upstairs.

It seemed as if she could see vague shadows all around her on the walls, that she knew weren't there at all. Had that detective done this to her—poisoned her mind with suspicion? Or. . . .

Archer reached for his hat the following morning, kissed her briefly, opened the door. " 'Bye. And don't forget to take your bath. I want to see you strong and husky, and the only way is to keep up those treatments daily."

"Sure you haven't overlooked anything this morning?" she called after him.

"Got everything this time. Just think, after we cash in on that ticket, I won't have to lug this brief-case and all these papers to work with me each morning. We'll celebrate tonight. And don't forget to take that bath."

Seconds after he had turned off their front walk, the

doorbell rang. Westcott must have been watching for him to leave, came around the side of the house, to get there that soon.

All her fears came back at sight of him; they showed plainly on her face. She stood aside sullenly. "I suppose you want to come in and go ahead trying to find a murder where there hasn't been any."

"That's as good a way to put it as any," he agreed somberly. "I won't keep you long; I know you're anxious to take your bath. I can hear the water running into the tub upstairs. He left a little later than his usual time this morning, didn't he?"

She eyed him in undisguised awe. "He did—but how did you know that?"

"He took a little longer to shave this morning, that's why."

This time she couldn't even answer, just gaped bewilderedly.

"Yes, I've been watching the house. Not only this morning, but ever since you arrived home last night. And at the odd times I've been called away by other matters, I've left someone in my place. From where I was posted, I had a fairly good view into your bathroom window. I could tell he—took longer to shave this morning. Can I go up there and look?"

Again she mutely stood aside, followed him up the stairs. The tiny tiled bathroom was already steamy with the water threatening to overflow the tub. Beside it stood an ultra-violet sun lamp, plugged into a wall outlet. He eyed both without touching either. What he did touch was a rolled-up tape measure resting on the hamper. He picked it up without a word, handed it back to her.

"I guess one of us left it in here," she said blankly. "It belongs——"

He had already started down the stairs again without waiting to hear her out. She took the precaution of turning off the taps first, then followed him down. He had gone on down into the basement, without asking her permission. He came up from there again a moment later and rejoined her at the back of the hall.

"Just trying to locate the control box that supplies the current to the house," he answered her questioning look.

She retreated a precautionary step. She didn't say anything, but he translated the fleeting thought that had just passed through her mind aloud. "No, I'm not insane. Maybe I am just a little touched; maybe a good detective, like a good artist or a good writer, has to be a little touched. Now we haven't very much time. Mr. Archer's almost certainly going to forget something again at the depot and come back. Before he does, just let me ask you two or three brief questions. You say Archer began to drop in quite frequently of an evening, shortly before Mead's death. They got quite pally."

"Yes indeed. Called each other by their first names and were on the best of terms. They'd sit chatting and nursing their highballs. Why, Stephen even brought Harry a present of some expensive whiskey two or three days before his death. That's how much he thought of him."

"Was that before or after Mead had this siege of indigestion that, according to corner or physician, resulted in his death?"

"Why, just before."

"I see. And it was quite an expensive whiskey. So expensive that Archer insisted on Mead's drinking it alone, wouldn't even share it with him: kept him company with some of Mead's common, ordinary, every day domestic rye," Westcott said.

Her face paled with surprise. "How did you know that?"

"I didn't. I do now."

"It was such a small quantity, in a little stone flagon, and he'd already sampled it himself at home before he brought it." She broke off short at the unmistakable, knowing look on his face. "I know what you're driving at! You're thinking Stephen poisoned him with it, aren't you? Last night it was a rifle bullet, this morning it's poison whiskey! Well, Mr. Detective, for your information, not a drop of that ever reached Harry's lips. I dropped the jug and lost it all over the kitchen floor while I was fixing their drinks for them. And I was ashamed and afraid to tell either one of them about it, after the way Stephen had been singing its praises, so I sent out for a bottle of ordinary Scotch and mixed the drinks with that instead, and they never knew the difference!"

"How do I know you're telling the truth?"

"I had a witness to the accident, that's how! The delivery man that brought the new bottle over from the liquor store saw me picking up the pieces all over the kitchen floor. He even shook his head and remarked what a shame it was, and pointed out that some of the rounded pieces of the jug still held enough liquor in their hollows for a man to get the makings of one good drink out of them! And then he helped me pick them up. Go ask him!"

"I think I would like to check with him. What store did he work for?"

"The Ideal, it's only a few blocks from here. And then be sure you come back and persecute my husband some more!" she flared.

"No, ma'am, I don't intend making a move against your husband. Any move that's made will have to come from him. And now, that's all the questioning I'm going to do, or need to do. I have my case all complete. And here he comes back—for something that he overlooked!"

A shadow blurred the plate glass insert of the front door, a key began to titillate in the lock. A low-pitched bleat of alarm was wrung from her. "No, you're going to arrest him!" Her hands went out appealingly toward his shoulders, to ward him off.

"I don't arrest people for things they haven't done. I'm leaving by the back door as he comes in the front. You run up and get in that tub—and let nature take its course. Hurry up, and not a word to him!"

She fled up the stairs like one possessed, wrapper fluttering after her like a parachute. A stealthy click from the back door, as Westcott let himself out, was drowned out by the opening of the front one, and Archer came in, wrangling the key that had delayed him, to get it out of the lock. A faint rippling of displaced water reached him from above.

He closed the door after him, advanced as far as the foot of the stairs, called up with perfect naturalness: "Josie! Got any idea where my iron pills are? I went off without them."

"Stephen! Again?" Her voice came down rebukingly. "I asked you when you left— And now I bet you've missed your train, too."

"What's the difference, I'll take the 9:22."

"They're in the sideboard in the dining-room, you know perfectly well." Her voice came down to him with metronome-like clarity, backed by the tiling around her as a sounding board.

"Can't hear you." He was half-way up the stairs by now. "Wait a minute, I'll come up."

His shuffling ascent of the stairs blotted out a second faint click from the direction of the back door, as though it had been left with its latch free instead of closed entirely, and a moment later Westcott's figure darted around the turn at the back of the hall and dove in swift silence through the basement door. He hastily wedged something under it to keep it ajar, then went on down the cellar steps.

"I said they're in the sideboard," she was still calling out.

But Archer was in the bathroom with her by this time. She was in a reclining position in the tub, hidden up to the chin by blue-green water. Modesty had made her sink lower in it at his entrance. The lighted sun lamp, backed by its burnished oblong reflector, cast a vivid violet-white halo down over her.

"Are you sure they're not in the medicine cabinet?" He crossed the tiny tiled cubicle toward it before she could answer. As he came abreast of the lamp, his elbow almost unnoticeably hitched outward, by no more than a fraction of an inch.

The long-stemmed lamp teetered, started to go over toward the brimming tub with almost hypnotic slowness.

"Stephen, the lamp!" she screamed warningly.

He had his back to her, was fumbling in the medicine cabinet. He didn't seem to hear her.

"The lamp!" she screamed a second time, more piercingly. That was all there was time for.

The violet-white had already dulled to orange, however, as it arched through the air. The orange dimmed to red. Then the water quenched it with a viperish hiss. The current seemed to have died out in it even before it went in.

He finally turned, at the sound of the splash, and faced her with perfect composure. It was only when he saw that she had jumped to her feet in the tub, snatched a towel to swathe around herself, and was trying to step back from the hissing lamp, that surprise showed in his face.

His eyes shot angrily and questioningly to the wall outlet at the other end of it. The cord was still plugged in. He stepped forward, pulled out the plug, replugged it—as though to re-establish contact if it had broken. She was still standing in water up to her knees. She didn't topple. Stood there erect, eyes wide open, fumblingly trying to lift the lamp with her one free hand.

The surprise on his face hardened into a sullen, lowering look of decision. The fingers of his two hands hooked in toward one another, in grasping position. The hands themselves slowly came up and out. He took a step forward, to reach her across the rim of the tub.

A voice said:

"O. K., you had your chance and you muffed it. Now put your hands into these—instead of where they were heading—before I kick out a few of your front teeth."

Westcott was standing in the bath doorway, one hand worrying a pair of handcuffs the way a man fiddles with a key ring or watch chain, the other hand half withdrawing a right angle of welded metal from over his hip.

Archer made an uncontrollable start forward, quickly checked it in time, as the right angle expanded into a pugnacious snub nose. He retreated as far as the small space would allow, then when he couldn't retreat any more, slumped there with the back of his neck up against the medicine chest mirror.

Mrs. Archer's reaction, toward this man who had just saved her life, was a typically feminine one. "Don't you dare come in here like this! Can't you see how I am?" She snatched a shower curtain around her to add to the towel.

"Sorry, little lady," Westcott said soothingly, keeping his eyes away from her with gentlemanly tact, "but it couldn't be helped. That was your murder just then." The handcuffs snapped hungrily around Archer's wrist, then his own. He went to the bath window, signaled to someone outside somewhere in the immediate vicinity of the house to come in.

"My murder!" gasped Mrs. Archer, who was simply a pair of eyes above the shower curtain by now.

"Sure. If I hadn't shut off the current in the house a split second after I heard you give that first warning scream—by throwing the master switch in the control box down in the basement—he would have had you electrocuted by now. The water around you in the tub would have been a perfect conductor. That's what he's been trying to do to you every time he knocked over that lamp.

"Don't you know what happens when a thing like that

lands in a tub of water, with you in the middle of it? The rim of the tub probably saved your life a couple of times, caught it too far up near the top and held it in a leaning position. Today he made sure it wouldn't by measuring off the distance between the lamp base and the tub rim, and setting it in close enough so that the filaments of the lamp would be bound to overreach the tub rim and go in the water. I watched him through the window. C'mon, you. Join us downstairs as soon as you're dressed, Mrs. Archer."

They were sitting there waiting for her in the living-room when she came down the stairs some time later, walking as though her knees were weak, bathrobe tightly gathered about her as though she were cold, and a stony, disillusioned look on her face. There was another man with Westcott, probably the assistant who had helped him keep watch on the house all night long.

Archer was saying sullenly to his captor as she entered the room: "D'you think you'll ever be able to convince my wife of that rigmarole you handed out upstairs?"

"I have already," Westcott answered. "Just look at her face."

"He has, Stephen," she said in a lifeless voice, slumping into a chair, shading her eyes, and shivering uncontrollably. "It happened too many times to be just a coincidence. You must have been trying to do something to me. Why did you *always* forget something and come back for it, just when I was in the tub? Why did the lamp *always* go over? And what was the tape measure from my sewing kit doing in the bathroom this morning? *I* didn't take it there." But she didn't look at him while she spoke, stared sadly down at the floor.

Archer's face darkened, he curled his lip sneeringly at her. "So that's the kind you are, ready to believe the first tinhorn cop that walks in here!" He turned angrily toward Westcott. "All right, you've poisoned her against me, you've got her on your side," he snarled, "but what'll it get you? You can't get me on a crime that wasn't even committed at all!"

Westcott walked toward his assistant. "What'd you find about that—anything?"

The other man silently handed him something written on a sheet of paper. Westcott read it over, then looked up, smiling a little.

"I can't get you on the crime that you wanted to commit and were prevented from just now. But I *can* get you on a crime you don't even *know* you committed, but that went through just the same. And that's the one I'm going to hook you on!"

He waved the paper on him. "One Tim McRae, employed as a messenger by the Ideal Liquor Store, died in agony several hours after he quit work and went home, on December 21st, 1939, this report says. It was thought to be accidental, from poisonous liquor, 'smoke,' at the time, and nothing was made of it.

"But I'm going to prove, with the help of Mrs. Archer here, and also through a casual remark McRae let drop to his employer, and which the latter didn't pay much attention to until now, that he scooped out dregs of liquor left in a broken flagon, that you brought into this house, offered to Harry Mead, and refused to touch yourself. I'm going to have McRae exhumed, and I think I'll find all the evidence I need in his vital organs. And I can tell by the look on your face that you think so, too!"

"Here's the taxi come to take us in to Headquarters. Let's just sum the whole thing up before we get started, shall we?

"Mead actually *did* die a natural death, of acute indigestion, aggravated by the shock of hearing an unexpected crash—probably some kids playing somewhere. So that clears the coroner of any dereliction of duty. But you thought all along you'd murdered him, because you knew damn well you'd brought in a poisoned jug of whiskey, and you thought he'd had some.

"She, the innocent party, came into his insurance, and you married her. That meant that she was the next one slated to go. You weren't going to try any more poisoning, even though you thought you'd gotten away with it the first time. That was asking for trouble, you felt.

"The electrocution in the bath gag was absolutely foolproof—if it had worked; you wouldn't have needed to worry about it afterwards. So you took it slow, to make sure it couldn't be proven to be anything but an accident. Who was going to prove that you'd been in the room at the time it happened? Who was going to prove that you'd given the lamp that little hitch with your elbow that sent it over? You would have left her shocked to death in the tub at 9:15 in the morning, and only 'discovered' her that way when you got back from work at five.

"Then the sweepstakes business came up in the middle of all this. That didn't stop you; you were conditioned to murder by that time. You decided to go ahead anyway. If it had been good for an 'accident' before she stood to win $150,000, it was even better for an 'accident' afterwards.

"Meanwhile, Mead's old-maid sister, who suspected all along there was something suspicious about his death—probably only because his widow married you instead of wearing sackcloth and ashes the rest of her life—came to us at Headquarters demanding an investigation, and I was quietly assigned to it.

"You were scared stiff to have Mead exhumed, fearful that your 'crime' might come to light in some unforeseen way. Fearful, maybe, we could tell by the condition of his body if he'd been poisoned. Something entirely different came to light. I found a wound on his temple— the skin broken and a bone in his head cracked. I thought at first that was it. It turned out not to be so at all.

"It was only when I went downtown and examined the coffin more closely, that I noticed the dent in it where it had been dropped after he was already in it. The under-taker's assistant, just a kid, broke down and told us the coffin had dropped when he'd been loading it into the hearse. It had fallen on the head part from the loading side. The fall banged the dead man's head against the side hard enough to break the skin and crack his skull.

"I questioned Mrs. Archer and she flew to your defense, and only managed to acquit herself, better than any lawyer could have, with a cock and bull tale of a flat-iron. But, accidentally, while on the trail of one murder, that it turned out had never been committed, I uncovered another, in process of being built up. In other words, what seemed to be a murder, but wasn't, fore-stalled a murder that was coming up.

"I can't get you for either of them. But when I pile the weight of both of them on top of the murder you actually *did* commit, but didn't know about until now, that of this Tim McRae, I can get you put away long enough so that there won't be a murder left in your system by the time you get out.

"Sort of crazy, isn't it? But sort of neat. Our cab's waiting."

THREE O'CLOCK

SHE HAD SIGNED HER own death-warrant. He kept telling himself over and over that he was not to blame, she had brought it on herself. He had never seen the man. He knew there was one. He had known for six weeks now. Little things had told him. One day he came home and there was a cigar-butt in an ashtray, still moist at one end, still warm at the other. There were gasoline-drippings on the asphalt in front of their house, and they didn't own a car. And it wouldn't be a delivery-vehicle, because the drippings showed it had stood there a long time, an hour or more. And once he had actually glimpsed it, just rounding the far corner as he got off the bus two blocks down the other way. A second-hand Ford. She was often very flustered when he came home, hardly seemed to know what she was doing or saying at all.

He pretended not to see any of these things; he was that type of man, Stapp, he didn't bring his hates or grudges out into the open where they had a chance to heal. He nursed them in the darkness of his mind. That's a dangerous kind of a man.

If he had been honest with himself, he would have had to admit that this mysterious afternoon caller was just the excuse he gave himself, that he'd daydreamed of getting rid of her long before there was any reason to, that there had been something in him for years past now urging Kill, kill, kill. Maybe ever since that time he'd been treated at the hospital for a concussion.

He didn't have any of the usual excuses. She had no money of her own, he hadn't insured her, he stood to gain nothing by getting rid of her. There was no other woman he meant to replace her with. She didn't nag and quarrel with him. She was a docile, tractable sort of wife. But this thing in his brain kept whispering Kill, kill, kill. He'd fought it down until six weeks ago, more from fear and a sense of self-preservation than from compunction. The discovery that there was some stranger calling on her in the afternoons when he was away, was all that had been needed to unleash it in all its hydra-headed ferocity. And the thought that he would be killing two instead of just one, now, was an added incentive.

So every afternoon for six weeks now when he came home from his shop, he had brought little things with him. Very little things, that were so harmless, so inoffensive, in themselves that no one, even had they seen them, could have guessed— Fine little strands of copper wire such as he sometimes used in his watch-repairing. And each time a very little package containing a substance that—well, an explosives expert might have recognized, but no one else. There was just enough in each one of those packages, if ignited, to go Fffft! and flare up like flashlight-powder does. Loose like that it couldn't hurt you, only burn your skin of course if you got too near it. But wadded tightly into cells, in what had formerly been a soap-box down in the basement, compressed to within an inch of its life the way he had it, the whole accumulated thirty-six-days worth of it (for he hadn't brought any home on Sundays)—that would be a different story. They'd never know. There wouldn't be enough left of the flimsy house for them to go by. Sewer-gas they'd think, or a pocket of natural gas in the ground somewhere around under them. Something like that had happened over on the other side of town two years ago, only not as bad of course. That had given him the idea originally.

He'd brought home batteries too, the ordinary dry-cell kind. Just two of them, one at a time. As far as the substance itself was concerned, where he got it was his business. No one would ever know where he got it. That was the beauty of getting such a little at a time like that. It wasn't even missed where he got it from. She didn't ask him what was in these little packages, because she didn't even see them, he had them in his pocket each time. (And of course he didn't smoke coming home.) But even if she had seen them, she probably wouldn't have asked him. She wasn't the nosey kind that asked questions, she would have thought it was watch-parts, maybe, that he brought home to work over at night or something. And then too she was so rattled and flustered herself these days, trying to cover up the fact that she'd had a caller, that he could have brought in a grandfather-clock under his arm and she probably wouldn't have noticed it.

Well, so much the worse for her. Death was spinning its web beneath her busy feet as they bustled obliviously back and forth in those ground-floor rooms. He'd be in his shop tinkering with watch-parts and the phone would ring. "Mr. Stapp, Mr. Stapp, your house has just been demolished by a blast!"

A slight concussion of the brain simplifies matters so beautifully.

He knew she didn't intend running off with this unknown stranger, and at first he had wondered why not. But by now he thought he had arrived at a satisfactory answer. It was that he, Stapp, was working, and the other man evidently wasn't, wouldn't be able to provide for her if she left with him. That must be it, what other reason could there be? She wanted to have her cake and eat it too.

So that was all he was good for, was it, to keep a roof over her head? Well, he was going to lift that roof sky-high, blow it to smithereens!

He didn't really want her to run off, anyway, that wouldn't have satisfied this thing within him that cried Kill, kill, kill. It wanted to *get* the two of them, and nothing short of that would do. And if he and she had had a five-year-old kid, say, he would have included the kid in the holocaust too, although a kid that age obviously couldn't be guilty of anything. A doctor would have known what to make of this, and would have phoned a hospital in a hurry. But unfortunately doctors aren't mind-readers and people don't go around with their thoughts placarded on sandwich-boards.

The last little package had been brought in two days ago. The box had all it could hold now. Twice as much as was necessary to blow up the house. Enough to break every window for a radius of blocks—only there were hardly any, they were in an isolated location. And that fact gave him a paradoxical feeling of virtue, as though he were doing a good deed; he was destroying his own but he wasn't endangering anybody else's home. The wires were in place, the batteries that would give off the necessary spark were attached. All that was necessary now was the final adjustment, the hook-up, and then—

Kill, kill, kill, the thing within him gloated.

Today was the day.

He had been working over the alarm-clock all morning to the exclusion of everything else. It was only a dollar-and-a-half alarm, but he'd given it more loving care than someone's Swiss-movement pocket-watch or platinum and diamond wristwatch. Taking it apart, cleaning it, oiling it, adjusting it, putting it together again, so that there was no slightest possibility of it failing him, of it not playing its part, of it stopping or jamming or anything else. That was one good thing about being your own boss, operating your own shop, there was no one over you to tell you what to do and what not to do. And he didn't have an apprentice or helper in the shop, either, to notice this peculiar absorption in a mere alarm-clock and tell someone about it later.

Other days he came home from work at five. This mysterious caller, this intruder, must be there from about two-thirty or three until shortly before she expected him. One afternoon it had started to drizzle at about a quarter to three, and when he turned in his doorway over two hours later there was still a large dry patch on the asphalt out before their house, just beginning to blacken over with the fine misty precipitation that was still falling. That was how he knew the time of her treachery so well.

He could, of course, if he'd wanted to bring the thing out into the open, simply have come an unexpected hour earlier any afternoon during those six weeks, and confronted them face to face. But he preferred the way of guile and murderous revenge; they might have had some explanation to offer that would weaken his purpose, rob him of his excuse to do the thing he craved. And he knew her so well, that in his secret heart he feared she would have if he once gave her a chance to offer it. Feared was the right word. He wanted to do this thing. He wasn't interested in a showdown, he was interested in a pay-off. This artificially-nurtured grievance had brought the poison in his system to a head, that was all. Without it it might have remained latent for another five years, but it would have erupted sooner or later anyway.

He knew the hours of her domestic routine so well that it was the simplest matter in the world for him to return to the house on his errand at a time when she would not be there. She did her cleaning in the morning. Then she had the impromptu morsel that she called lunch. Then she went out, in the early afternoon, and did her marketing for their evening meal. They had a phone in the house but she never ordered over it; she liked, she often told him, to see what she was getting, otherwise the tradespeople simply foisted whatever they chose on you, at their own prices. So from one until two was the time for him to do it, and be sure of getting away again unobserved afterwards.

At twelve-thirty sharp he wrapped up the alarm-clock in ordinary brown paper, tucked it under his arm, and left his shop. He left it every day at this same time to go to his own lunch. He would be a little longer getting back today, that was all. He locked the door carefully after him, of course; no use taking chances, he had too many valuable watches in there under repair and observation.

He boarded the bus at the corner below, just like he did every day when he was really going home for the night. There was no danger of being recognized or identified by any bus-driver or fellow-passenger or anything like that, this was too big a city. Hundreds of people used these busses night and day. The drivers didn't even glance up at you when you paid your fare, déftly made change for you backhand by their sense of touch on the coin you gave them alone. The bus was practically empty, no one was going out his way at this hour of the day.

He got off at his usual stop, three interminable suburban blocks way from where he lived, which was why his house had not been a particularly good investment when he bought it and no others had been put up around it afterwards. But it had its compensations on such a day as this. There were no neighbors to glimpse him returning to it at this unusual hour, from their windows, and remember that fact afterwards. The first of the three blocks he had to walk had a row of taxpayers on it, one-story store-fronts. The next two were absolutely vacant from corner to corner, just a panel of advertising billboards on both sides, with their gallery of friendly people that beamed on him each day twice a day. Incurable optimists these people were; even today when they were going to be shattered and splintered they continued to grin and smirk their counsel and messages of cheer. The perspiring bald-headed fat man about to quaff some non-alcoholic beverage. "The pause that refreshes!" The grinning colored laundress hanging up wash. "No ma'am, I just uses a little Oxydol." The farmwife at the rural telephone sniggering over her shoulder: "Still talking about their new Ford 8!" They'd be tatters and kindling in two hours from now, and they didn't have sense enough to get down off there and hurry away.

"You'll wish you had," he whispered darkly as he passed by beneath them, clock under arm.

But the point was, that if ever a man walked three "city" blocks in broad daylight unseen by the human eye, he did that now. He turned in the short cement walk when he came to his house at last, pulled back the screen door, put his latchkey into the wooden inner door and let himself in. She wasn't home, of course; he'd known she wouldn't be, or he wouldn't have come back like this.

He closed the door again after him, moved forward into the blue twilight-dimness of the inside of the house. It seemed like that at first after the glare of the street. She had the green shades down three-quarters of the way on all the windows to keep it cool until she came back. He didn't take his hat off or anything, he wasn't staying. Particularly after he once set this clock he was carrying in motion. In fact it was going to be a creepy feeling even walking back those three blocks to the bus-stop and standing waiting for the bus to take him downtown again, knowing all the time something was going *tick-tock, tick-tock* in the stillness back here, even though it wouldn't happen for a couple of hours yet.

He went directly to the door leading down to the basement. It was a good stout wooden door. He passed through it, closed it behind him, and went down the bare brick steps to the basement-floor. In the winter, of course, she'd had to come down here occasionally to regulate the oil-burner while he was away, but after the fifteenth of April no one but himself ever came down here at any time, and it was now long past the fifteenth of April.

She hadn't even known that he'd come down, at that. He'd slipped down each night for a few minutes while she was in the kitchen doing the dishes, and by the time she got through and came out, he was upstairs again behind his newspaper. It didn't take long to add the contents of each successive little package to what was already in the box. The wiring had taken more time, but he'd gotten that done one night when she'd gone out to the movies (so she'd said—and then had been very vague about what the picture was she'd seen, but he hadn't pressed her.)

The basement was provided with a light-bulb over the stairs, but it wasn't necessary to use it except at night; daylight was admitted through a horizontal slit of window that on the outside was flush with the ground, but on the inside was up directly under the basement-ceiling. The glass was wire-meshed for protection and so cloudy with lack of attention as to be nearly opaque.

The box, that was no longer merely a box now but an infernal machine, was standing over against the wall, to one side of the oil-burner. He didn't dare shift it about any more now that it was wired and the batteries inserted. He went over to it and squatted down on his heels before it, and put his hand on it with a sort of loving gesture. He was proud of it, prouder than of any fine watch he'd ever repaired or reconstructed. A watch, after all, was inanimate. This was going to become animate in a few more minutes, maybe diabolically so, but animate just the same. It was like—giving birth.

He unwrapped the clock and spread out the few necessary small implements he'd brought with him from the shop on the floor beside him. Two fine copper wires were sticking stiffly out of a small hole he'd bored in the box, in readiness, like the antennæ of some kind of insect. Through them death would go in.

He wound the clock up first, for he couldn't safely do that once it was connected. He wound it up to within an inch of its life, with a professionally deft economy of wrist-motion. Not for nothing was he a watch-repairer. It must have sounded ominous down in that hushed basement, to hear that *crick-craaaack, crick-craaaack*, that so-domestic sound that denotes going to bed, peace, slumber, security; that this time denoted approaching annihilation. It would have if there'd been any listener. There wasn't any but himself. It didn't sound ominous to him, it sounded delicious.

He set the alarm for three. But there was a difference now. Instead of just setting off a harmless bell when the hour hand reached three and the minute hand reached twelve, the wires attached to it leading to the batteries would set off a spark. A single, tiny, evanescent spark— that was all. And when that happened, all the way downtown where his shop was, the showcase would vibrate, and maybe one or two of the more delicate watch-mechanisms would stop. And people on the streets would stop and ask one another: "What was that?"

They probably wouldn't even be able to tell definitely, afterwards, that there'd been anyone else beside herself in the house at the time. They'd know that she'd been there only by a process of elimination; she wouldn't be anywhere else afterwards. They'd know that the house had been there only by the hole in the ground and the litter around.

He wondered why more people didn't do things like this; they didn't know what they were missing. Probably not clever enough to be able to make the things themselves, that was why.

When he'd set the clock itself by his own pocket-watch—1:15—he pried the back off it. He'd already bored a little hole through this at his shop. Carefully he

guided the antenna-like wires through it, more carefully
still he fastened them to the necessary parts of the mechanism without letting a tremor course along them. It was
highly dangerous but his hands didn't play him false,
they were too skilled at this sort of thing. It wasn't vital
to reattach the back to the clock, the result would be the
same if it stood open or closed, but he did that too, to
give the sense of completion to the job that his crafts-
man's soul found necessary. When he had done with it, it
stood there on the floor, as if placed there at random up
against an innocent-looking copper-lidded soapbox,
ticking away. Ten minutes had gone by since he had
come down here. One hour and forty minutes were still
to go by.

Death was on the wing.

He stood up and looked down at his work. He
nodded. He retreated a step across the basement floor,
still looking down, and nodded again, as if the slight
perspective gained only enhanced it. He went over to the
foot of the stairs leading up, and stopped once more and
looked over. He had very good eyes. He could see the
exact minute-notches on the dial all the way over where
he now was. One had just gone by.

He smiled a little and went on up the stairs, not fur-
tively or fearfully but like a man does in his own house,
with an unhurried air of ownership, head up, shoulders
back, tread firm.

He hadn't heard a sound over his head while he was
down there, and you could hear sounds quite easily
through the thin flooring, he knew that by experience.
Even the opening and closing of doors above could be
heard down here, certainly the footsteps of anyone walking about in the ground-floor rooms if they bore down
with their normal weight. And when they stood above
certain spots and spoke, the sound of the voices and even
what was said came through clearly, due to some trick of

acoustics. He'd heard Lowell Thomas clearly, on the radio, while he was down here several times.

That was why he was all the more unprepared, as he opened the basement door and stepped out into the ground-floor hall, to hear a soft tread somewhere up above, on the second floor. A single, solitary footfall, separate, disconnected, like Robinson Crusoe's foot-print. He stood stockstill a moment, listening tensely, thinking—hoping, rather, he'd been mistaken. But he hadn't. The slur of a bureau-drawer being drawn open or closed reached him, and then a faint tinkling sound as though something had lightly struck one of the glass toilet-articles on Fran's dresser.

Who else could it be but she? And yet there was a stealth to these vague disconnected noises that didn't sound like her. He would have heard her come in; her high heels usually exploded along the hardwood floors like little firecrackers.

Some sixth sense made him turn suddenly and look behind him, toward the dining-room, and he was just in time to see a man, half-crouched, shoulders bunched forward, creeping up on him. He was still a few yards away, beyond the dining-room threshold, but before Stapp could do more than drop open his mouth with reflex astonishment, he had closed in on him, caught him brutally by the throat with one hand, flung him back against the wall, and pinned him there.

"What are you doing here?" Stapp managed to gasp out.

"Hey, Bill, somebody *is* home!" the man called out guardedly. Then he struck out at him, hit him a stunning blow on the side of the head with his free hand. Stapp didn't reel because the wall was at the back of his head, that gave him back the blow doubly, and his senses dulled into a whirling flux for a minute.

Before they had cleared again, a second man had

leaped down off the stairs from one of the rooms above, in the act of finishing cramming something into his pocket.

"You know what to do, hurry up!" the first one ordered. "Get me something to tie him with and let's get out of here!"

"For God's sake, don't tie—!" Stapp managed to articulate through the strangling grip on his windpipe. The rest of it was lost in a blur of frenzied struggle on his part, flailing out with his legs, clawing at his own throat to free it. He wasn't fighting the man off, he was only trying to tear that throttling impediment off long enough to get out what he had to tell them, but his assailant couldn't tell the difference. He struck him savagely a second and third time, and Stapp went limp there against the wall without altogether losing consciousness.

The second one had come back already with a rope, it looked like Fran's clothesline from the kitchen, that she used on Mondays. Stapp, head falling forward dazedly upon the pinioning arm that still had him by the jugular, was dimly aware of this going around and around him, crisscross, in and out, legs and body and arms.

"Don't—" he panted. His mouth was suddenly nearly torn in two, and a large handkerchief or rag was thrust in, effectively silencing all further sound. Then they whipped something around outside of that, to keep it in, and fastened it behind his head. His senses were clearing again, now that it was too late.

"Fighter, huh?" one of them muttered grimly. "What's he protecting? The place is a lemon, there's nothing in it."

Stapp felt a hand spade into his vest-pocket, take his watch out. Then into his trouser-pocket and remove the little change he had on.

"Where'll we put him?"

"Leave him where he is."

THREE O'CLOCK 87

"Naw. I did my last stretch just on account of leaving a guy in the open where he could put a squad-car on my tail too quick; they nabbed me a block away. Let's shove him back down in there where he was."

This brought on a new spasm, almost epileptic in its violence. He squirmed and writhed and shook his head back and forth. They had picked him up between them now, head and feet, kicked the basement door open, and were carrying him down the steps to the bottom. They still couldn't be made to understand that he wasn't resisting, that he wouldn't call the police, that he wouldn't lift a finger to have them apprehended—if they'd only let him get out of here, *with* them.

"This is more like it," one said, as they deposited him on the floor. "Whoever lives in the house with him won't find him so quick—"

Stapp started to roll his head back and forth on the floor like something demented, toward the clock, then toward them, toward the clock, toward them. But so fast that it finally lost all possible meaning, even if it would have had any for them in the first place, and it wouldn't have of course. They still thought he was trying to free himself in unconquerable opposition.

"Look at that!" one of them jeered. "Did you ever see anyone like him in your life?" He backed his arm threateningly at the wriggling form. "I'll give you one that'll hold you for good, if you don't cut it out!"

"Tie him up to that pipe over there in the corner," his companion suggested, "or he'll wear himself out rolling all over the place." They dragged him backwards along the floor and lashed him in a sitting position, legs out before him, with an added length of rope that had been coiled in the basement.

Then they brushed their hands ostentatiously and started up the basement stairs again, one behind the other, breathing hard from the struggle they'd had with

him. "Pick up what we got and let's blow," one muttered.
"We'll have to pull another one tonight—and this time
you let *me* do the picking!"

"It looked like the berries," his mate alibied. "No one
home, and standing way off by itself like it is."

A peculiar sound like the low simmering of a tea-kettle
or the mewing of a newborn kitten left out in the rain to
die came percolating thinly through the gag in Stapp's
mouth. His vocal cords were strained to bursting with
the effort it was costing him to make even that slight
sound. His eyes were round and staring, fastened on
them in horror and imploring.

They saw the look as they went on up, but couldn't
read it. It might have been just the physical effort of
trying to burst his bonds, it might have been rage and
threatened retribution, for all they knew.

The first passed obliviously through the basement
doorway and passed from sight. The second stopped
halfway to the top of the stairs and glanced complacently
back at him—the way he himself had looked back at his
own handiwork just now, short minutes ago.

"Take it easy," he jeered, "relax. I used to be a sailor.
You'll never get out of *them* knots, buddy."

Stapp swiveled his skull desperately, threw his eyes at
the clock one last time. They almost started out of their
sockets, he put such physical effort into the look.

This time the man got it finally, but got it wrong. He
flung his arm at him derisively. "Trying to tell me you
got a date? Oh no you haven't, you only think you have!
Whadda you care what time it is, *you*'re not going any
place!"

And then with the horrible slowness of a nightmare—
though it only seemed that way, for he resumed his
ascent fairly briskly—his head went out through the
doorway, his shoulders followed, his waist next. Now
even optical communication was cut off between them,
and if only Stapp had had a minute more he might have

made him understand! There was only one backthrust foot left in sight now, poised on the topmost basement step to take flight. Stapp's eyes were on it as though their burning plea could hold it back. The heel lifted up, it rose, trailed through after the rest of the man, was gone.

Stapp heaved himself so violently, as if to go after it by sheer will-power, that for a moment his whole body was a distended bow, clear of the floor from shoulders to heels. Then he fell flat again with a muffled thud, and a little dust came out from under him, and a half-dozen little separate skeins of sweat started down his face at one time, crossing and intercrossing as they coursed. The basement door ebbed back into its frame and the latch dropped into its socket with a minor click that to him was like the crack of doom.

In the silence now, above the surge of his own tidal breathing that came and went like surf upon a shoreline, was the counterpoint of the clock. Tick-tick, tick-tick, tick-tick, tick-tick.

For a moment or two longer he drew what consolation he could from the knowledge of their continued presence above him. An occasional stealthy footfall here and there, never more than one in succession, for they moved with marvelous dexterity, they must have had a lot of practice in breaking and entering. They were very cautious walkers from long habit even when there was no further need for it. A single remark filtered through, from somewhere near the back door. "All set? Let's take it this way." The creak of a hinge, and then the horrid finality of a door closing after them, the back door, which Fran may have forgotten to lock and by which they had presumably entered in the first place; and then they were gone.

And with them went his only link with the outside world. They were the only two people in the whole city who knew where he was at this moment. No one else, not a living soul, knew where to find him. Nor what would happen to him if he wasn't found and gotten out of here by three o'clock. It was twenty-five to two now. His discovery of their presence, the fight, their trussing him up with the rope, and their final unhurried departure, had all taken place within fifteen minutes.

It went tick-tick, tick-tock; tick-tick, tick-tock, so rhythmically, so remorselessly, so *fast*.

An hour and twenty-five minutes left. Eighty-five minutes left. How long that could seem if you were waiting for someone on a corner, under an umbrella, in the rain—like he had once waited for Fran outside the office where she worked before they were married, only to find that she'd been taken ill and gone home early that day. How long that could seem if you were stretched out on a hospital-bed with knife-pains in your head and nothing to look at but white walls, until they brought your next tray—as he had been that time of the concussion. How long that could seem when you'd finished the paper, and one of the tubes had burned out in the radio, and it was too early to go to bed yet. How short, how fleeting, how instantaneous, that could seem when it was all the time there was left for you to live in and you were going to die at the end of it!

No clock had ever gone this fast, of all the hundreds that he'd looked at and set right. This was a demon-clock, its quarter-hours were minutes and its minutes seconds. Its lesser hand didn't even pause at all on those notches the way it should have, passed on from one to the next in perpetual motion. It was cheating him, it wasn't keeping the right time, somebody slow it down at least if nothing else! It was twirling like a pinwheel, that secondary hand.

Tick-tock-tick-tock-tick-tock. He broke it up into "Here I go, here I go, here I go."

There was a long period of silence that seemed to go on forever after the two of them had left. The clock told him it was only twenty-one minutes. Then at four to two a door opened above without warning—oh blessed sound, oh lovely sound!—the front door this time (over above *that* side of the basement), and high-heeled shoes clacked over his head like castanets.

"Fran!" he shouted. "Fran!" he yelled. "Fran!" he screamed. But all that got past the gag was a low whimper that didn't even reach across the basement. His face was dark with the effort it cost him, and a cord stood out at each side of his palpitating neck like a splint.

The tap-tap-tap went into the kitchen, stopped a minute (she was putting down her parcels; she didn't have things delivered because then you were expected to tip the errand-boys ten cents), came back again. If only there was something he could kick at with his interlocked feet, make a clatter with. The cellar-flooring was bare from wall to wall. He tried hoisting his lashed legs clear of the floor and pounding them down again with all his might; maybe the sound of the impact would carry up to her. All he got was a soft, cushioned sound, with twice the pain of striking a stone surface with your bare palm, and not even as much distinctness. His shoes were rubber-heeled, and he could not tilt them up and around far enough to bring them down on the leather part above the lifts. An electrical discharge of pain shot up the backs of his legs, coursed up his spine, and exploded at the back of his head, like a brilliant rocket.

Meanwhile her steps had halted about where the hall closet was (she must be hanging up her coat), then went on toward the stairs that led to the upper floor, faded out upon them, going up. She was out of earshot now, temporarily. But she was in the house with him at least! That awful aloneness was gone. He felt such gratitude for her nearness, he felt such love and need for her, he wondered how he could ever have thought of doing away with her—only one short hour ago. He saw now that he must have been insane to contemplate such a thing. Well if he had been, he was sane now, he was rational now, this ordeal had brought him to his senses. Only release him, only rescue him from his jeopardy, and he'd never again . . .

Five-after. She'd been back nine minutes now. There, it was ten. At first slowly, then faster and faster, terror, which had momentarily been quelled by her return, began to fasten upon him again. Why did she stay up there on the second floor like that? Why didn't she come down here to the basement, to look for something? Wasn't there anything down here that she might suddenly be in need of? He looked around, and there wasn't. There wasn't a possible thing that might bring her down here. They kept their basement so clean, so empty. Why wasn't it piled up with all sorts of junk like other people's! That might have saved him now.

She might intend to stay up there all afternoon! She might lie down and take a nap, she might shampoo her hair, she might do over an old dress. Any one of those trivial harmless occupations of a woman during her husband's absence could prove so fatal now! She might count on staying up there until it was time to begin getting his supper ready, and if she did—no supper, no she, no he.

Then a measure of relief came again. The man. The man whom he had intended destroying along with her, *he* would save him. He would be the means of his salvation. He came other days, didn't he, in the afternoon, while Stapp was away? Then, oh God, let him come today, make this one of the days they had a rendezvous (and yet maybe it just wasn't!). For if he came, that would bring her down to the lower floor, if only to admit him. And how infinitely greater his chances would be, with two pairs of ears in the house to overhear some wisp of sound he might make, than just with one.

And so he found himself in the anomalous position of a husband praying, pleading with every ounce of fervency he can muster, for the arrival, the materialization, of a rival whose existence he had only suspected until now, never been positive of.

Eleven past two. Forty-nine minutes left. Less than the time it took to sit through the "A"-part of a picture-show. Less than the time it took to get a haircut, if you had to wait your turn. Less than the time it took to sit through a Sunday meal, or listen to an hour program on the radio, or ride on the bus from here to the beach for a dip. Less than all those things—to live. No, no, he had been meant to live thirty more years, forty! What had become of those years, those months, those weeks? No, not just *minutes* left, it wasn't fair!

"Fran!" he shrieked. "Fran, come down here! Can't you hear me?" The gag drank it up like a sponge.

The phone trilled out suddenly in the lower hallway, midway between him and her. He'd never heard such a beautiful sound before. "Thank God!" he sobbed, and a tear stood out in each eye. That must be the man now. That would bring her down.

Then fear again. Suppose it was only to tell her that he wasn't coming? Or worse still, suppose it was to ask her instead to come out and meet him somewhere else? Leave him alone down here, once again, with this horror ticking away opposite him. No child was ever so terrified of being left alone in the dark, of its parents putting out the light and leaving it to the mercy of the boogy-man as this grown man was at the thought of her going out of the house and leaving him behind.

It kept on ringing a moment longer, and then he heard her quick step descending the stairs to answer it. He could hear every word she said down there where he was. These cheap matchwood houses.

"Hello? Yes, Dave. I just got in now."

Then, "Oh Dave, I'm all upset. I had seventeen dollars upstairs in my bureau-drawer and it's gone, and the wrist-watch that Paul gave me is gone too. Nothing else is missing, but it looks to me as if someone broke in here while I was out and robbed us."

Stapp almost writhed with delight down there where he was. She knew they'd been robbed! She'd get the police now! Surely they'd search the whole place, surely they'd look down here and find him!

The man she was talking to must have asked her if she was sure. "Well, I'll look again, but I know it's gone. I know just where I left it, and it isn't there. Paul will have a fit."

No Paul wouldn't either; if she'd only come down here and free him he'd forgive her anything, even the cardinal sin of being robbed of his hard-earned money.

Then she said, "No, I haven't reported it yet. I suppose I should, but I don't like the idea—on your account, you know. I'm going to call up Paul at the shop. There's just a chance that he took the money and the watch both with him when he left this morning. I remember telling him the other night that it was losing time; he may have wanted to look it over. Well, all right, Dave, come on out then."

So he was coming, so Stapp wasn't to be left alone in the place; hot breaths of relief pushed against the sodden gag at the back of his palate.

There was a pause while she broke the connection. Then he heard her call his shop-number, "Trevelyan 4512," and wait while they were ringing, and of course no one answered.

Tick-tick, tick-tick, tick-tick.

The operator must have told her finally that they couldn't get the number. "Well, keep ringing," he heard her say, "it's my husband's store, he's always there at this hour."

He screamed in terrible silence: "I'm right here under your feet! Don't waste time! For God's sake, come away from the phone, come down here!"

Finally, when failure was reported a second time, she hung up. Even the hollow, cupping sound of that detail reached him. Oh, everything reached him—but help. This was a torture that a Grand Inquisitor would have envied.

He heard her steps move away from where the phone was. Wouldn't she guess by his absence from where he was supposed to be that something was wrong? Wouldn't she come down here now and look? (Oh, where was this woman's intuition they spoke about?!) No, how could she be expected to. What connection could the basement of their house possibly have in her mind with the fact that he wasn't in his shop? She wasn't even alarmed, so far, by his absence most likely. If it had been evening; but at this hour of the day— He might have gone out later than other days to his lunch, he might have had some errand to do.

He heard her going up the stairs again, probably to resume her search for the missing money and watch. He whimpered disappointedly. He was as cut off from her, while she remained up there, as if she'd been miles away, instead of being vertically over him in a straight line.

Tick, tock, tick, tock. It was twenty-one past two now. One half-hour and nine scant minutes more left. And they ticked away with the prodigality of tropical rain-drops on a corrugated tin roof.

He kept straining and pulling away from the pipe that held him fast, then falling back exhausted, to rest awhile, to struggle and to strain some more. There was as recurrent a rhythm to it as there was to the ticking of the clock itself, only more widely spaced. How could ropes hold that unyieldingly? Each time he fell back weaker, less able to contend with them than the time before. For he wasn't little strands of hemp, he was layers of thin skin that broke one by one and gave forth burning pain and finally blood.

The doorbell rang out sharply. The man had come. In

less than ten minutes after their phone talk he had reached the house. Stapp's chest started rising and falling with renewed hope. Now his chances were good again. Twice as good as before, with two people in the house instead of only one. Four ears instead of two, to hear whatever slight sound he might manage to make. And he must, he must find a way of making one. He gave the stranger his benediction while he stood there waiting to be admitted. Thank God for this admirer or whatever he was, thank God for their rendezvous. He'd give them his blessing if they wanted it, all his worldly goods; anything, anything, if they'd only find him, free him.

She came quickly down the stairs a second time and her footfalls hurried down the hall. The front door opened. "Hello, Dave," she said, and he heard the sound of a kiss quite clearly. One of those loud unabashed ones that bespeak cordiality rather than intrigue.

A man's voice, deep, resonant, asked: "Well, did it turn up yet?"

"No, and I've looked high and low," he heard her say. "I tried to get Paul after I spoke to you, and he was out to lunch."

"Well, you can't just let seventeen dollars walk out the door without lifting your finger."

For seventeen dollars they were standing there frittering his life away—and their own too, for that matter, the fools!

"They'll think I did it, I suppose," he heard the man say with a note of bitterness.

"Don't say things like that," she reproved. "Come in the kitchen and I'll make you a cup of coffee."

Her quick brittle step went first, and his heavier, slower one followed. There was the sound of a couple of chairs being drawn out, and the man's footfalls died out entirely. Hers continued busily back and forth for a while, on a short orbit between stove and table.

What were they going to do, *sit* up there for the next

half-hour? Couldn't he *make* them hear in some way? He tried clearing his throat, coughing. It hurt furiously, because the lining of it was all raw from long strain. But the gag muffled even the cough to a blurred purring sort of sound.

Twenty-six to three. Only minutes left now, minutes; not even a full half-hour any more.

Her footsteps stopped finally and one chair shifted slightly as she joined him at the table. There was linoleum around the stove and sink that deadened sounds, but the middle part of the room where the table stood was ordinary pine-board flooring. It let things through with crystalline accuracy.

He heard her say, "Don't you think we ought to tell Paul about—us?"

The man didn't answer for a moment. Maybe he was spooning sugar, or thinking about what she'd said. Finally he asked, "What kind of a guy is he?"

"Paul's not narrow-minded," she said. "He's very fair and broad."

Even in his agony, Stapp was dimly aware of one thing: that didn't sound a bit like her. Not her speaking well of him, but that she could calmly, detachedly contemplate broaching such a topic to him. She had always seemed so proper and slightly prudish. This argued a sophistication that he hadn't known she'd had.

The man was evidently dubious about taking Paul into their confidence, at least he had nothing further to say. She went on, as though trying to convince him: "You have nothing to be afraid of on Paul's account, Dave, I know him too well. And don't you see, we can't keep on like this? It's better to go to him ourselves and tell him about you, than wait until he finds out. He's liable to think something else entirely, and keep it to himself, brood, hold it against me, unless we explain. I know that he didn't believe me that night when I helped you find a furnished room, and told him I'd been to a

movie. And I'm so nervous and upset each time he comes
home in the evening, it's a wonder he hasn't noticed it
before now. Why I feel as guilty as if—as if I were one of
these disloyal wives or something." She laughed embar-
rassedly, as if apologizing to him for even bringing such
a comparison up.

What did she mean by that?

"Didn't you ever tell him about me at all?"

"You mean in the beginning? Oh, I told him you'd
been in one or two scrapes, but like a little fool I let him
think I'd lost track of you, didn't know where you were
any more."

Why, that was her brother she'd said that about!

The man sitting up there with her confirmed it right as
the thought burst in his mind. "I know it's tough on you,
Sis. You're happily married and all that. I've got no right
to come around and gum things up for you. No one's
proud of a jailbird, an escaped convict, for a brother—"

"David," he heard her say, and even through the flooring there was such a ring of earnestness in her voice
Stapp could almost visualize her reaching across the
table and putting her hand reassuringly on his, "there
isn't anything I wouldn't do for you, and you should
know that by now. Circumstances have been against
you, that's all. You shouldn't have done what you did,
but that's spilt milk and there's no use going back over it
now."

"I suppose I'll have to go back and finish it out. Seven
years, though, Fran, seven years out of a man's life—"

"But this way you have no life at all—"

Were they going to keep on talking his life away?
Nineteen to three. One quarter of an hour, and four
minutes over!

"Before you do anything, let's go downtown and talk
it over with Paul, hear what he says." One chair jarred
back, then the other. He could hear dishes clatter, as

though they'd all been lumped together in one stack. "I'll do these when I come back," she remarked.

Were they going to leave again? Were they going to leave him behind here, alone, with only minutes to spare?

Their footsteps had come out into the hall now, halted a moment undecidedly. "I don't like the idea of you being seen with me on the streets in broad daylight, you could get in trouble yourself, you know. Why don't you phone him to come out here instead?"

Yes, yes, Stapp wailed. Stay with me! Stay!

"I'm not afraid," she said gallantly. "I don't like to ask him to leave his work at this hour, and I can't tell him over the phone. Wait a minute, I'll get my hat." Her footsteps diverged momentarily from his, rejoined them again.

Panic-stricken, Stapp did the only thing he could think of. Struck the back of his head violently against the thick pipe he was attached to.

A sheet of blue flame darted before his eyes. He must have hit one of the welts where he had already been struck once by the burglars. The pain was so excruciating he knew he couldn't repeat the attempt. But they must have heard something, some dull thud or reverberation must have carried up along the pipe. He heard her stop short for a minute and say, "What was that?"

And the man, duller-sensed than she and killing him all unknowingly, "What? I didn't hear anything."

She took his word for it, went on again, to the hall-closet to get her coat. Then her footsteps retraced themselves all the way back through the dining-room to the kitchen. "Wait a minute, I want to make sure this back door's shut tight. Locking the stable after the horse is gone!"

She came forward again through the house for the last time, there was the sound of the front door opening, she passed through it, the man passed through it, it closed, and they were gone. There was the faint whirr of a car starting up outside in the open.

And now he was left alone with his self-fashioned doom a second time, and the first seemed a paradise in retrospect compared to this, for then he had a full hour to spare, he had been rich in time, and now he only had fifteen minutes, one miserly quarter-hour.

There wasn't any use struggling any more. He'd found that out long ago. He couldn't anyway, even if he'd wanted to. Flames seemed to be licking lazily around his wrists and ankles.

He'd found a sort of palliative now, the only way there was left. He'd keep his eyes down and pretend the hands were moving slower than they were, it was better than watching them constantly, it blunted a little of the terror at least. The ticking he couldn't hide from. Of course every once in a while when he couldn't resist looking up and verifying his own calculations, there'd be a renewed burst of anguish, but in-between-times it made it more bearable to say, "It's only gained a half-minute since the last time I looked." Then he'd hold out as long as he could with his eyes down, but when he couldn't stand it any more and would have to raise them to see if he was right, it had gained *two* minutes. Then he'd have a bad fit of hysterics, in which he called on God, and even on his long-dead mother, to help him, and couldn't see straight through the tears. Then he'd pull himself together again, in a measure, and start the self-deception over again. "It's only about thirty seconds now since I last looked. . . . Now it's about a minute . . ." (But was it? But was it?) And so on, mounting slowly to another climax of terror and abysmal collapse.

Then suddenly the outside world intruded again, that world that he was so cut off from that it already seemed as far-away, as unreal, as if he were already dead. The doorbell rang out.

He took no hope from the summons at first. Maybe some peddler—no, that had been too aggressive to be a peddler's ring. It was the sort of ring that claimed admission as its right, not as a favor. It came again. Whoever was ringing was truculently impatient at being kept waiting. A third ring was given the bell, this time a veritable blast that kept on for nearly half-a-minute. The party must have kept his finger pressed to the bell-button the whole time. Then as the peal finally stopped, a voice called out forcefully: "Anybody home in there? Gas Company!" And suddenly Stapp was quivering all over, almost whinnying in his anxiety.

This was the one call, the one incident in all the day's domestic routine, from earliest morning until latest night, that could have possibly brought anyone down into the basement! The meter was up there on the wall, beside the stairs, staring him in the face! And her brother had had to take her out of the house at just this particular time! There was no one to let the man in.

There was the impatient shuffle of a pair of feet on the cement walk. The man must have come down off the porch to gain perspective with which to look inquiringly up at the second-floor windows. And for a fleeting moment, as he chafed and shifted about out there before the house, on the walk and off, Stapp actually glimpsed the blurred shanks of his legs standing before the grimy transom that let light into the basement at ground-level. All the potential savior had to do was crouch down and peer in through it, and he'd see him tied up down there. And the rest would be so easy!

Why didn't he, why didn't he? But evidently he didn't expect anyone to be in the basement of a house in which his triple ring went unanswered. The tantalizing trouser-leg shifted out of range again, the transom became blank. A little saliva filtered through the mass of rag in Stapp's distended mouth, trickled across his silently vibrating lower lip.

The gas inspector gave the bell one more try, as if venting his disappointment at being balked rather than in any expectation of being admitted this late in the proceedings. He gave it innumerable short jabs, like a telegraph-key. Bip-bip-bip-bip-bip. Then he called out disgustedly, evidently for the benefit of some unseen assistant waiting in a truck out at the curb, "They're never in when you want 'em to be!" There was a single quick tread on the cement, away from the house. Then the slur of a light truck being driven off.

Stapp died a little. Not metaphorically, literally. His arms and legs got cold up to the elbows and knees, his heart seemed to beat slower, and he had trouble getting a full breath; more saliva escaped and ran down his chin, and his head drooped forward and lay on his chest for awhile, inert.

Tick-tick, tick-tick, tick-tick. It brought him to after awhile, as though it were something beneficient, smelling salts or ammonia, instead of being the malevolent thing it was.

He noticed that his mind was starting to wander. Not much, as yet, but every once in a while he'd get strange fancies. One time he thought that his *face* was the clock-dial, and that thing he kept staring at over there was his face. The pivot in the middle that held the two hands became his nose, and the 10 and the 2, up near the top, became his eyes, and he had a red-tin beard and head of hair and a little round bell on the exact top of his crown for a hat. "Gee, I look funny," he sobbed drowsily. And he caught himself twitching the muscles of his face, as if trying to stop those two hands that were clasped on it before they progressed any further and killed that man over there, who was breathing so metallically: tick, tock, tick, tock.

Then he drove the weird notion away again, and he saw that it had been just another escape-mechanism. Since he couldn't control the clock over there, he had attempted to change it into something else. Another vagary was that this ordeal had been brought on him as punishment for what he had intended doing to Fran, that he was being held fast there not by the inanimate ropes but by some active, punitive agency, and that if he exhibited remorse, pledged contrition to a proper degree, he could automatically effect his release at its hands. Thus over and over he whined in the silence of his throttled throat, "I'm sorry. I won't do it again. Just let me go this one time, I've learned my lesson, I'll never do it again."

The outer world returned again. This time it was the phone. It must be Fran and her brother, trying to find out if he'd come back here in their absence. They'd found the shop closed, must have waited outside of it for a while, and then when he still didn't come, didn't know what to make of it. Now they were calling the house from a booth down there, to see if he had been taken ill, had returned here in the meantime. When no one answered, that would tell them, surely, that something was wrong. Wouldn't they come back now to find out what had happened to him?

But why should they think he was here in the house if he didn't answer the phone? How could they dream he was in the basement the whole time? They'd hang around outside the shop some more waiting for him, until as time went on, and Fran became real worried, maybe they'd go to the police. (But that would be hours from now, what good would it do?) They'd look everywhere but here for him. When a man is reported missing the last place they'd look for him would be in his own home.

It stopped ringing finally, and its last vibration seemed to hang tenuously on the lifeless air long after it had ceased, humming outward in a spreading circle like a pebble dropped into a stagnant pool. *Mmmmmmmmm*, until it was gone, and silence came rolling back in its wake.

She would be outside the pay-booth or wherever it was she had called from, by this time. Rejoining her brother, where he had waited. Reporting, "He's not out at the house either." Adding the mild, still unworried comment, "Isn't that strange?. Where on earth can he have gone?" Then they'd go back and wait outside the locked shop, at ease, secure, unendangered. She'd tap her foot occasionally in slight impatience, look up and down the street while they chatted.

And now *they* would be two of those casuals who would stop short and say to one another at three o'clock: "What was that?" And Fran might add, "It sounded as though it came from out our way." That would be the sum-total of their comment on his passing.

Tick, tock, tick, tock, tick, tock. Nine minutes to three. Oh, what a lovely number was nine. Let it be nine forever, not eight or seven, nine for all eternity. Make time stand still, that he might breathe though all the world around him stagnated, rotted away. But no, it was already eight. The hand had bridged the white gap between the two black notches. Oh, what a precious number was eight, so rounded, so symmetrical. Let it be eight forever—

A woman's voice called out in sharp reprimand, somewhere outside in the open: "Be careful what you're doing, Bobby, you'll break a window!" She was some distance away, but the ringing dictatorial tones carried clearly.

Stapp saw the blurred shape of a ball strike the basement-transom, he was looking up at it, for her voice had come in to him through there. It must have been just a tennis-ball, but for an instant it was outlined black against the soiled pane, like a small cannonball; it seemed to hang there suspended, to adhere to the glass, then it dropped back to the ground. If it had been ordinary glass it might have broken it, but the wire-mesh had prevented that.

The child came close up against the transom to get its ball back. It was such a small child that Stapp could see its entire body within the height of the pane, only the head was cut off. It bent over to pick up the ball, and then its head came into range too. It had short golden ringlets all over it. Its profile was turned toward him, looking down at the ball. It was the first human face he'd seen since he'd been left where he was. It looked like an angel. But an inattentive, unconcerned angel.

It saw something else while it was still bent forward close to the ground, a stone or something that attracted it, and picked that up too and looked at it, still crouched over, then finally threw it recklessly away over its shoulder, whatever it was.

The woman's voice was nearer at hand now, she must be strolling along the sidewalk directly in front of the house. "Bobby, stop throwing things like that, you'll hit somebody!"

If it would only turn its head over this way, it could look right in, it could see him. The glass wasn't too smeary for that. He started to weave his head violently from side to side, hoping the flurry of motion would attract it, catch its eye. It may have, or its own natural curiosity may have prompted it to look in without that. Suddenly it had turned its head and was looking directly in through the transom. Blankly at first, he could tell by the vacant expression of its eyes.

Faster and faster he swiveled his head. It raised the heel of one chubby, fumbling hand and scoured a little clear spot to squint through. Now it could see him, now surely! It still didn't for a second. It must be much darker in here than outside, and the light was behind it.

The woman's voice came in sharp reproof: "Bobby, what are you doing there?!"

And then suddenly it saw him. The pupils of its eyes shifted over a little, came to rest directly on him. Interest replaced blankness. Nothing is strange to children—not

a man tied up in a cellar any more than anything else—
yet everything is. Everything creates wonder, calls for
comment, demands explanation. Wouldn't it say anything to her? Couldn't it talk? It must be old enough to;
she, its mother, was talking to it incessantly. "Bobby,
come away from there!"

"Mommy, look!" it said gleefully.

Stapp couldn't see it clearly any more, he was shaking
his head so fast. He was dizzy, like you are when you've
just gotten off a carousel; the transom and the child it
framed kept swinging about him in a half-circle, first too
far over on one side, then too far over on the other.

But wouldn't it understand, wouldn't it understand
that weaving of the head meant he wanted to be free?
Even if ropes about the wrists and ankles had no meaning to it, if it couldn't tell what a bandage around
the mouth was, it must know that when anyone writhed
like that they wanted to be let loose. Oh God, if it had
only been two years older, three at the most! A child of
eight, these days, would have understood and given
warning.

"Bobby, are you coming? I'm waiting!"

If he could only hold its attention, keep it rooted there
long enough in disobedience to her, surely she'd come
over and get it, see him herself as she irritably sought to
ascertain the reason for its fascination.

He rolled his eyes at it in desperate comicality, winked
them, blinked them, crossed them. An elfin grin peered
out on its face at this last; already it found humor in a
physical defect, or the assumption of one, young as it
was.

An adult hand suddenly darted downward from the
upper right-hand corner of the transom, caught its wrist,
bore its arm upward out of sight. "Mommy, look!" it
said again, and pointed with its other hand. "Funny
man, tied up."

The adult voice, reasonable, logical, dispassionate—

inattentive to a child's fibs and fancies—answered: "Why that wouldn't look nice, Mommy can't peep into other people's houses like you can."

The child was tugged erect at the end of its arm, its head disappeared above the transom. Its body was pivoted around, away from him; he could see the hollows at the back of its knees for an instant longer, then its outline on the glass blurred in withdrawal, it was gone. Only the little clear spot it had scoured remained to mock him in his crucifixion.

The will to live is an unconquerable thing. He was more dead than alive by now, yet presently he started to crawl back again out of the depths of his despair, a slower longer crawl each time, like that of some indefatigable insect buried repeatedly in sand, that each time manages to burrow its way out.

He rolled his head away from the window back toward the clock finally. He hadn't been able to spare a look at it during the whole time the child was in sight. And now to his horror it stood at three to three. There was a fresh, a final blotting-out of the burrowing insect that was his hopes, as if by a cruel idler lounging on a beach.

He couldn't *feel* any more, terror or hope or anything else. A sort of numbness had set in, with a core of gleaming awareness remaining that was his mind. *That* would be all that the detonation would be able to blot out by the time it came. It was like having a tooth extracted with the aid of novocaine. There remained of him now only this single pulsing nerve of premonition; all the tissue around it was frozen. So protracted foreknowledge of death was in itself its own anaesthetic.

Now it would be too late even to attempt to free him first, before stopping the thing. Just time enough, if someone came down those stairs this very minute, sharp-edged knife with which to sever his bonds already in hand, for him to throw himself over toward it, reverse it.

And now—now it was too late even for that, too late for anything but to die.

He was making animal-noises deep in his throat as the minute hand slowly blended with the notch of twelve. Guttural sounds like a dog worrying a bone, though the gag prevented their emerging in full volume. He puckered the flesh around his eyes apprehensively, creased them into slits—as though the closing of his eyes could ward off, lessen, the terrific force of what was to come! Something deep within him, what it was he had no leisure nor skill to recognize, seemed to retreat down long dim corridors away from the doom that impeded. He hadn't known he had those convenient corridors of evasion in him, with their protective turns and angles by which to put distance between himself and menace. Oh clever architect of the Mind, oh merciful blueprints that made such emergency exits available. Toward them this something, that was he and yet not he, rushed; toward sanctuary, security, toward waiting brightness, sunshine, laughter.

The hand on the dial stayed there, upright, perpendicular, a perfect right-angle to its corollary, while the swift seconds that were all there were left of existence ticked by and were gone. It wasn't so straight now any more, but he didn't know it, he was in a state of death already. White reappeared between it and the twelve-notch, *behind* it now. It was one minute after three. He was shaking all over from head to foot—not with fear, with laughter.

It broke into sound as they plucked the dampened, bloodied gag out, as though they were drawing the laughter out after it, by suction or osmosis.

"No, don't take those ropes off him yet!" the man in the white coat warned the policeman sharply. "Wait'll they get here with the straitjacket first, or you'll have your hands full."

Fran said through her tears, cupping her hands to her ears, "Can't you stop him from laughing like that? I can't stand it. Why does he keep laughing like that?"

"He's out of his mind, lady," explained the intern patiently.

The clock said five past seven. "What's in this box?" the cop asked, kicking at it idly with his foot. It shifted lightly along the wall a little, and took the clock with it.

"Nothing," Stapp's wife answered, through her sobs and above his incessant laughter. "Just an empty box. It used to have some kind of fertilizer in it, but I took it out and used it on the flowers I--I've been trying to raise out in back of the house."

CHANGE OF MURDER

He who hesitates is caught

Brains DONLEAVY, EARLY ONE Chicago evening, set out to call upon his friend Fade Williams. He was dressed for the occasion in a dark blue hourglass overcoat, eyebrow-level derby, and armpit-cuddling .38. It being a windy evening he would have caught cold without any one of the three, particularly the last.

He and Fade had known each other for years. They had so much on each other they were of necessity the best of friends; the .38 therefore was just habit and not precaution. Fade, to be accurate, was not the given name of the gent. Although he had been known to vanish, disappear into thin air, for long stretches at a time, his nickname didn't derive from that trait either. It was borrowed from a game of chance, the lowly pastime of shooting craps, in which the expression "fade" means one player is willing to match the other's stake—put up an equal amount—in other words, back the hazard.

Not that Fade ever played craps; there were bigger and better ways of earning money. He was a semi-professional alibi doctor, a backstop, a set-up arranger. Although good stiff fees figured in his adroit juggling of times, places and circumstances, his amateur standing must be granted; he wasn't listed in the telephone red book and he had no shingle out advertising his services. He had to know you; you couldn't just walk in off the street, plank down a retainer and walk out with an alibi all neatly done up in brown paper. A too-frequent appearance in the witness chair, helping to clear persons "mistakenly" accused of committing crime, might have caused Justice to squint suspiciously at Fade after awhile.

But Fade's batting-average was consistently good, that arranging a deal with him was almost like buying immunity at the outset. Which was why Brains Donleavy was on his way to him right then, having a murder in mind.

Brains would have been indignant to hear it called that. With him it was just "getting squared up." Murder was the name for other people's killings, not his. Not one of the half-a-dozen he already had to his credit had lacked cause or justice as he saw it. He never killed simply for the sake of killing, nor even for profit; it was just that he had an almost elephantine faculty for holding grudges.

Yet relentless as he could be about wiping out old scores, there was also a wide streak of sentimentality in his make-up. "Mother Machree" could bring tears to his eyes if his beer had been needled enough. He had been known to pitch rocks through butcher-shop windows in the dead of night simply to release the imprisoned kittens locked behind them. Anyway, he found his way into one of the lesser honky-tonks that infest the Loop district, the designation "The Oasis" flaming above it in red tube-letters. It was not a club or cabaret, simply a beer-garden used by Fade as a front. A radio provided what entertainment there was. The bartender tilted his head to inquire "Waddle it be?"

"It'll be the boss," said Brains. "Tell him Donleavy."

The bartender didn't move from the spot, just bent over as if to take a look at what stock he had lined up below the bar. His lips moved soundlessly, he straightened up, and a thumb popped out of his balled fist.

"Straight through the back," he said. "See that door there?"

Brains did and went toward it. Before he quite made it, it opened and Fade was standing there to welcome him.

"How's the boy?" he said hospitably.

"I got something I gotta talk over with you," said Brains.

"Sure," said Fade, "come right in." He guided him through with an affectionate arm about his shoulder, looked back to scan the outside of the establishment once more, then closed the door after them.

There was a short passageway with a telephone-booth on each side of it, ending at the open door of Fade's office. The booth on the left-hand side had a sign dangling from it, "Out of order." In brushing by, Brains dislodged it and it fell down. Fade carefully picked it up and replaced it before following him in. Then he closed the office door after them.

"Well," he said, "how d'ye like my new place? Nifty, ain't it?"

Brains looked around. On the desk that Fade had recently been sitting at lay a .38, broken open. Near it was a scrap of soiled chamois rag, and a little pile of the bullets that had come out of the gun. Brains smiled humorlessly. "Weren't expecting trouble, were you?" he asked.

"I always do that, like to fiddle around with 'em, keep 'em clean," explained Fade. "Helps me pass the time away, sitting in here by the hour like I do. I've got quite a few hanging around, sometimes I take 'em out and look 'em over—makes me think of the old days." He sat down, scooped up the bullets in the hollow of his hand, and began to replace them in the gun one by one. "What's on your mind?" he said, poring over his task.

Brains abruptly sat down opposite him. "Listen, I got

a little squaring-up set for tomorrow night," he began
confidentially. "You be the doctor, will ya? Set me up
good and foolproof—"

"A rub-out?" asked Fade without even looking up at
him. "What, again?"

"Why, I haven't raised a rod to no one in eighteen
months," protested Brains virtuously.

"Maybe so, but you was in stir the first twelve, or so
they tell me. Why don't you lay off once in awhile, give it
a rest?"

"I wasn't up for no rub-out," contradicted Brains,
"you oughta know that; you squared my last one for me.
They got me for knocking down an old lady one time I
was practising learning to drive a pal's car."

Fade clicked the reloaded gun shut and put it down.

"Which reminds me," he remarked, getting up and
going over to a small wall-safe, "I think I got something
coming to me on that Cincinnati cover-up I done for
you."

"Sure," agreed Brains placidly, tapping an inner
pocket. "I got the do-re-mi with me right now."

Fade apparently wasn't taking his word for it unsupported; he opened the little built-in strongbox, drew out
a cluttered handful of papers, and scanned them one by
one.

"Yeah, here it is," he said. "One-fifty, made out to look
like a gambling debt. You gave me the other one-fifty the
night before, remember?" He thrust the rest back into
the safe, brought it over to the desk with him—without,
however, taking his hand off it.

Brains was laboriously counting out ten-spots, moistening his thumb. He pushed the heap across the desk
when he was through. "There y'go—"

"Want me to tear this up for you?" offered Fade, edg-
ing the I.O.U. forward with one hand, pulling the money
toward him with the other.

"I'll tear it up myself," remarked Brains. He looked at

it, folded it, and carefully put it away. "It might slip your mind." Neither one showed any animosity. "Now, how about it?" he went on. "Will you cover me for tomorrow night?"

Fade picked up the .38 and the rag once more, went back to cleaning it.

"You're getting to be a bad risk, Brains," he murmured between puffs of breath on the metal. "Once or twice it's a pushover, but you're starting to go in for it too often. If I keep popping up in front of you each time, it starts to look bad for me; they were already smelling a rat in Cincinnati that time, kept coming around questioning me for weeks afterwards." He went on scouring lovingly for awhile. "It's gonna take five hundred this time, if I do it for you," he let his client know. "It keeps getting tougher to make it look right all the time."

"Five hundred!" exclaimed Brains heatedly. "You must be screwy! For five hundred I could go out and get half-a-dozen guys paid off, without having to do it myself!"

Fade jerked his head impassively toward the door. "Then go ahead, why come to me?" Brains made no move to get up and leave, however. "You know as well as me," Fade told him, "whoever you hired would loosen up in the first station-house back room they brought him to. And another thing," he added shrewdly, "it's the satisfaction of doing it yourself you're after."

Brains nodded vigorously. "Sure. Who the hell wants to git squared up by remote control? I like t'see their eyes when they lamp the slug with their name on it coming outa the gat. I like t'see them fall and turn over, kinda slow the way they do—" He shuffled through the remainder of the money he was holding. "Give ya a century now," he offered, "that's all I got left on me. I guarantee ya the other four hundred the minute the heat goes down. You couldn't expect the full amount beforehand anyway; nobody does business that way."

He slithered the money enticingly under Fade's down-turned palm. "What d'ya say?" he urged. "It's a pushover, a natural—you can fix me up with one hand tied behind your back." And by way of professional flattery, "I coulda got him in Gary last week already, but I kept my hands down. I wouldn't pull it without one of your outs to back me."

Fade put down his cleaning-rag, snapped the wad of bills back and forth a couple of times under his thumb-nail, finally wacked them against the edge of the desk by way of consent.

"Gimme a little dope on it," he said gruffly. "And make it your last for a while, will ya? I'm no Houdini."

Brains hitched his chair forward eagerly. "What my reason is, is poisonal. This guy has stomped all over my pet corns. You don't needa know who he is and I ain't telling ya. I followed him there from Gary early in the week, like I said, and I been keeping close tabs on him ever since. He ain't even expecting nothing to happen to him, which is what's so beautiful about it." He clasped his hands, spit between them, and rubbed them together, eyes beaming. "He's at a rat-hole on the North Side, and the way the layout is, he's practically begging for it. I been drawing diagrams all week and I got it by heart." He took out pencil and paper and began to scratch away. Fade leaned forward interestedly, cautioning, "Keep your voice down."

"It's seven stories high and he's got a room on the top floor. Now I don't even have to go in and out or pass anybody to get at him, see? The winder of his room looks out on an air shaft that dents in the side wall. There's no fire-escape—nothing—just a drain-pipe running up and down the shaft. Now across the shaft is a six-story tenement-flat smack up against the hotel. It's such a cheesy place they don't even keep the roof door locked, you can walk right up from the street. I been up there all week, lying flat on my belly looking into his room. I got a plank hidden away up there right now, waiting for me to use it to get across on. I even measured it across to his window ledge while he was out of his room, and it reaches with lots of room left over. He's on the seventh floor, the flat's six stories high, so the roof is only about a yard above the top of his winder, there ain't even enough incline to the plank to make it hard getting back across again—" He spread his hands triumphantly. "I plug him through one of these big Idaho potatoes, and they won't even hear it happen in the next room, much less out on the street!"

Fade dug at his nose judiciously. "It's got points in its favor and it's got points against it," he submitted. "Watch yourself on that plank business, remember what happened that time at Hopewell."

"I didn't even bring it in the house with me," gloated Brains. "It was half off and I yanked it outa the backyard fence."

"Suppose he sees you coming across on it; won't he duck outa the room?"

"I'm getting in while he's out, I'll be laying for him in the closet when he comes back. He leaves his winder open from the bottom each time to get air in the room."

"How about other windows on a line with his? Somebody might squint out and happen to get a look at you crossing over."

"There's no dent in the wall of the flat, so there's no winders on that side at all. On the hotel side there's just one winder to a floor on the shaft, all straight under his. The room under him's been vacant since day before yesterday—no one there to see. From the fifth floor down I don't think they could see the plank that far away against the night sky; it's painted dark green and the shaft is a buzzard for darkness. That's my end of it and it's a lulu. Now let's hear your end, showing how I wasn't even there at all to do it!"

"How much time you want?" Fade asked.

"I can be there and back and leave him lying stretched out cold behind me in thirty minutes," said Brains.

"I'll give you an hour, starting from here and coming back here," clipped Fade. "Now sign this I.O.U., and then pay close attention. If it goes wrong you've only got yourself to blame."

Brains read the slip of paper Fade had filled out. Like the last transaction of this kind between them, it was disguised as a simple gambling debt and had absolutely no legal value. It didn't have to have. Brains knew what the penalty for welshing on one of those haphazard little scraps of writing would have been. It had no time limit, but Fade was surer of collecting on it in the end than a creditor backed to the hilt by all the legal red tape ever devised.

Brains laboriously scrawled "Brains Donleavy" at the bottom of it, mouth open, and returned it. Fade put it in the safe along with the hundred cash, closed it without bothering to lock it.

"Now come outside the door with me a minute," he said. "I wanna show you something."

In the passageway between the two phone booths he said, "Get this and hang onto it; you're paying five hundred for it: There's no way in or out of my office except through the front, like you came in. No windows, nothing. Once you're in, you're in—until everyone outside there sees you come out again." He dug his elbow into Brains' ribs. "But here's how you leave—and here's how you come back in again when you're all squared-up over there."

He unhitched the "Out of Order" sign, tucked it under his arm, and folded back the glass slide of the booth. "Step in," he invited, "like you was gonna call up somebody—and shove hard against the back wall of the booth."

Brains did so—and nearly fell out into the open on his ear; the wall was hinged like a door. He took a quick look around him, saw that he was at the back of a dimly-lighted garage. The nearest light-bulb was yards away. The outside of the door was whitewashed to blend with the plaster of the walls; the battered hulk of an old car, with the wheels removed, was standing in such a way that it formed a screen for the peculiar exit.

Brains got back in again, the door swung to after him. He stepped out of the booth, Fade closed it and hung the sign back in place.

"I own the garage," he mentioned, "but just the same don't let the guy out there see you come through. He ain't hep to it; neither is the bartender on this side. The booth's a dummy I had built for myself."

"Kin it open from the outside for you to get back again?" Brains wanted to know.

"No, leave a little wedge of cardboard under it on your way out, like a shoehorn," Fade told him, "but not wide enough for any light to shine through. Now, what time you showing up here?"

"Ten," said Brains. "He always gets in the same time each night, round ten-thirty."

"Okay," said Fade briskly. "You ask for me out front, like tonight. I come out there and we slap each other on the back, toss off a couple together. Then we wander back here and somehow we get into a friendly little game of two-handed draw poker. I send out for more drinks and the barman brings 'em in and sees us both in here, in our shirtsleeves. We yell a lot at each other, so that everybody in the place can hear us—I'll see that the radio ain't going. Then we quiet down, and that's when you duck out. I'll raise a howl every once in awhile, like you was still in here with me. After you get back, we both stroll out again and I see you to the door. You won heavy, see, and to prove it you stand everyone in the place a drink before you go—they'll remember you by that alone, don't worry. There's your set-up."

Brains looked at him admiringly. "Kid," he said, "it's

worth close to five hundred at that, the way you tell it!"

"Hell," said Fade lugubriously, "I ain't making enough profit on it you could sneeze at—installin' that fake booth alone come to near a hundred-fifty."

He sat down at the desk once more, took up the .38 and rag, and resumed his fancy work. "Another thing, if you're riding back, zig-zag and change cabs. Don't give 'em a chance to trace you in a straight line back to the garage. I own it, like I told you." He squinted down the bore of the gun toward the handle, blew his breath along it.

"Watch y'self, you reloaded that thing," Brains warned jumpily. "One of these days you're gonna blow your own head off monkeying around that way. Well, I'm gonna go home and get a good night's rest so I can enjoy myself t'morra night." He saluted from his eyebrow and departed.

"S'matta wit the radio, don't it work?" a barfly was asking the following evening when Brains walked in. An unusual silence hung over "The Oasis," although they were lined up two deep before the mirror.

"It's gotta go to the repair-shop," answered the bartender curtly. He saw Brains coming and ducked below the counter without waiting to be told, put his mouth to the speaking-tube Fade had rigged up between the bar and his office. The back door opened and Fade came out, booming cordial greetings. Every head turned that way.

Fade and Brains each slung an arm to the other's shoulder, made a place for themselves at the rail.

"Set 'em up for my pal Donleavy," ordered Fade. Brains tried to pay. "Naw, this is my house," protested Fade.

Several minutes of this at the top of their voices, and the bartender slung a pair of dice down before them. They clicked busily for awhile, idle eyes watching every move. Finally Fade cast them from him impatiently.

"Y'got my blood up now," he confessed. "I know a better way than this of getting back atcha! C'mon back in the office, I'll go you a few rounds with the cards." The door closed behind them.

"They'll be in there all night," said the bartender knowingly.

Once they were behind the door all their labored cordiality vanished. They went to work in cold-blooded silence. Fade stripped the stamp off a new deck of cards, strewed them across the table. He sluiced off coat and vest, hung them on a peg; Brains likewise, revealing his shoulder-holster. They each grabbed up five cards at random, sat down at opposite sides of the desk.

"Jack," muttered Fade, tapping the table. Brains hauled out a fistful of change and singles, flung it down between them. They both relaxed, scanned their hands.

"Play with what y'got," mouthed Fade, "he'll be in with the drinks in a minute."

The second door, between the office and the phone booths, had been left open. Brains flipped down two cards, reached for two more. The outside door suddenly opened and the barman came in with two glasses and a bottle on a tray. He left it open behind him, and they were in full sight of those at the bar for a few minutes. He put down the bottle and glasses, then paused to glance noisily over his employer's shoulder. His eyes widened; Fade was holding a royal flush, it had just happened that way.

"Scram," the latter remarked curtly, "and don't come back in again. I gotta concentrate!"

The man edged out with the empty tray, closed the outer door after him, and went back to tell the customers about the phenomenal luck his boss was having.

Fade instantly turned his hand around so Brains could see it.

"Raise a racket," he commanded, "and get going!

Don't forget the wedge under the booth or you won't get in again."

Brains was busy shovelling on vest, coat, and topcoat and buttoning himself into them. He banged his fist down on the desk with enough force to shatter it and let loose a roar of startled profanity. Fade matched him bellow for bellow; both their faces were stonily impassive.

"I'll let out a howl every once in awhile like you was still in here with me," Fade promised.

Brains downed his drink, clasped his own hands together and shook them at him, pushed back the door of the booth with the "Out of Order" sign on it, and sandwiched himself into it. He closed it, tore the cover off a folder of matches and pleated it together, then pushed the hinged door ajar on the other side of him and slipped through. The wedge held it on a crack; there was just room enough to get a nail-hold.

The back of the garage was steeped in gloom. He edged forward around the derelict chassis and peered ahead. The single attendant was way out front at the entrance, standing talking to the owner of a car that had just driven in.

Brains skittered along toward them, but stayed close to the wall, screened by a long row of parked cars, bending double to bridge the gap between each one and the next. One had been run in too close to the wall; he had to climb the rear bumper and run along it like a monkey to get by. The last car in line, however, was still a good fifteen or twenty yards from the mouth of the garage, and there was a big, bare, gasoline-soaked stretch between him and the open street ahead. He skulked waiting where he was, in the shadow cast by the last car. In about a minute more the customer went away on foot, the mechanic got in the car and drove it past Brains' hiding-place to the back of the garage. It was an ideal chance to leave unseen, better than he'd thought he'd get. He straightened up, sprinted across the remaining stretch of concrete, turned from sight at the entrance, and went walking unhurriedly down the street.

At the second corner he came to, he got into a cab, and got out again half-way to his destination. He went into a store, asked the price of a fountain pen, came out again and got into another cab. This time he got out two blocks from where he was going, at right angles to it. The cab went one way and he went the other, around the corner. He headed straight for the dingy flat, as though he lived in it; didn't look around him going in and above all didn't make the mistake of passing it the first time and then doubling back.

There was no one out on the stoop to watch him go by. He pushed the unlocked door in and went trudging slowly up the stairs, just like anyone coming home tired. Everything was with him tonight, he didn't even meet anyone the whole six flights, although the place was a beehive of noise.

Someone came out and went down, but that was after he was two floors above. After the top landing, he put the soft pedal on his trudge and quickened it. The roof door, latched on the inside, didn't squeak any more; he'd oiled the hinges himself two nights before. He eased it shut behind him and found himself out in the dark, moving silently across graveled tar. The plank was still there where he'd left it, on the opposite side from where he was going to use it, so no one seeing it in the daytime would connect it with the hotel window across the air shaft. He brought it over, set it down, flattened himself on his stomach, and peered over the edge.

He treated himself to a one-cornered smile. The room behind the window was dark, its occupant hadn't come in yet. The lower pane was open a foot from the bottom, to get a little air in. Just the way he'd told Fade it would be! The window below was blank; they hadn't rented that room yet since last night. Even the second and third ones down were dark; there wasn't a light above the third floor, and this far up it showed no bigger than a postage stamp. The whole layout was made to order.

He got up on his knees, hauled the plank across the low lead coping, and began to pay it out aimed at the window. He kept pressure on it at his end with one foot so it wouldn't sink below the windowledge in midair with his own weight. It crossed the ledge without touching it and pushing the curtains back under the open window. Then he let it down very slowly and carefully and the gap was bridged. He made sure it extended far back enough over the coping, lest it slip off after he was on it; then he let go of it, brushed his hands, stood up, and stepped up on it where it rested on the coping. He balanced himself gingerly.

He wasn't worried about it snapping under his weight; he'd tested it plenty before now on the roof itself. He bent down on it, grasped one edge with each hand, and started across it on hands and knees. The distance wasn't great, and he kept from looking down, fastened his eyes on the window just ahead. There was a very slight incline, but not enough to bother him. He saw to it that it didn't tip by keeping his weight in the middle as much as possible. In fact, he had everything down pat— couldn't miss. The window pane came to meet him until it lay cold across the tip of his nose. He hooked his hands onto the bottom of it, flung it the rest of the way up, and corkscrewed down under it into the room. It had been as easy as all that!

The first thing he did was lower it again behind him to its original level. He shoved the board back a little so the dent it made wouldn't be so noticeable against the curtains, but left it in place. He didn't have to put the lights on; he'd memorized the exact position of every article of furniture in the room from his vantage point on the roof opposite. He opened the closet door, shoved the clothes on their hangers a little to one side to make room for himself. Then he took the .38 out from under his arm, went over to the room door, and stood listening. There wasn't a sound from outside. He reached in his topcoat pocket and pulled out a large raw potato with a small hole carefully bored through it. He jammed this onto the muzzle of his gun for a silencer, tight enough so it wouldn't fall off. Then he sat down for awhile on a chair in the dark, holding it in his hand and peering toward the door.

After about fifteen minutes an elevator-door clashed open somewhere in the distance. He got right up, stepped backwards into the closet, and swung the door to in front of him. He left it on a slight crack, a thread of visibility, just enough for one eye to see through. That one-cornered smile had come back on his face. A key jiggled in the room door. It opened, and someone's black outline showed against the lighted hall. It closed again and the lights went up in the room.

For a split second the face that turned was in a line with the crack of the closet door, and Brains nodded to himself; the right guy had come home to the right room, and the last possible, but unlikely, hitch to his plan was safely out of the way—he'd come home alone.

Then the face passed on out of focus. The key clashed down on the glass bureau top, an edge of a dark coat fell across the white bed, and there was a click and a midget radio started to warm up with a low whine. The guy yawned once out loud, moved around a little out of sight. Brains just stood there waiting, muffled gun in hand.

When it came it was quick as the flash of a camera shutter. The closet door was suddenly wide open and they were staring into each other's faces, not more than six inches apart. The guy's one hand was still on the doorknob, the other was holding up his coat ready to hang. He dropped that first of all. Brains didn't even bring the gun up, it was already in position. The guy's face went from pink to white to gray, and sort of slid loose like jelly ready to fall off his skull. He took a very slow step back to keep from falling, and Brains took a very slow step out after him. He kicked the guy's coat out of the way without looking at it.

"Well, Hitch," he said softly, "the first three out have your name on 'em. Close your eyes if you want to."

Hitch didn't; instead they got big and round as hard-boiled eggs with their shells off. His mouth and tongue moved for a whole minute without getting anything off. Finally three words formed. "What's it for?"

Brains only heard them because he was so close.

"Keep turning slowly around while I remind you," he said, "paws loose like a dog begging for a bone."

As the victim tottered around in one place like a top riding for a fall, hands dangling downward at shoulder level, Brains deftly slapped him in just the right number of places to make sure he was unarmed.

"All right," he acquiesced, "that was the last exercise you'll be taking."

The other man stopped rotating, buckled a little at the knees, then just hung there as if he was suspended from a cord.

The toy radio finally got through its warming up, the whine faded out of it, and a third voice entered the room, tinny and blurred. Brains' eyes flickered over that way for an instant, then back to the doughy face in front of him.

"I get out of stir six months ago," he snarled, "and the first thing I do is come back looking for my last year's frail—they call her Goldie—you used to see me with her, remember?"

Hitch's eyes began rolling around in his face like buckshot.

"No sign of Goldie anywhere," resumed Brains, "so I ask around, and what do I hear? That a rat named Hitch, who was supposed to be a friend of mine, had stepped up and walked off with Goldie while my back is turned. Now get me right"—he motioned the gun slightly—"it ain't the dame that's troubling me; they got no sense anyway and I wouldn't want her now even if I could have her—but no guy does that to me and gets way with it. Don't matter if it's business, or a dame, or just passing remarks about me I don't like, anyone that crowds me, this is how I git squared up."

The creases across the knuckle of his trigger-finger began to smooth out as it started bending back; Hitch's eyes were on them, dilated like magnifying glasses. "Don't I get a word in?" he said hoarsely.

"It won't do ya no good," Brains promised, "but go ahead, let's hear ya try to lie out of it—the same answer'll still be ready for ya behind this spud."

Hitch began to shake all over, in his anxiety to get the greatest number of words out of his system in the shortest possible length of time. "I ain't gonna lie, you've got me and what good would it do? She was starving," he yammered, "the cash you left with her run out on her—" Even in the midst of the panic that gripped him his eyes found time to gauge Brains' reaction to this. "I know you left her well-heeled but—but somebody lifted it, cleaned her out," he corrected. "She came to me, and she didn't have the price of a meal on her, didn't have a roof over her. I—I started looking after her, on account of you was my friend—"

Brains snorted disgustedly. Sweat was pouring down Hitch's face. The voice on the radio had been replaced by thin weepy strains of music now. Again Brains' eyes shifted to it, lingered for a minute, then came back again.

"Wouldn'tcha have done that for anyone yourself?" Hitch pleaded. "Wouldn'tcha have done that yourself?

Then, without meaning to, I guess we kinda fell for each other—"

Brains didn't bat an eye, but the gun was pointed a little lower, at the victim's thigh now, not his chest; the weight of the potato may have done that. Hitch's head had followed it down, his eyes were on it; he seemed to be staring contritely at the floor.

"We knew we was wrong. We talked it over lots; we both said how swell you was—" A shade of color had returned to his face; it was still pale but no longer gray. He kept swallowing, it could have been either overpowering emotion or the need for keeping his throat well-lubricated. "Finally we give in—we just couldn't help it—we got married—" A slight sob thickened his voice.

For the first time Brains showed some surprise; his mouth opened a little and stayed that way. Hitch seemed to find inspiration in the pattern of the hotel rug that met his eyes.

"Not only that but—but Goldie has a kid now. We have a little baby—" He looked up ruefully. "We named it after you—" The gun was pointing straight down at the floor now; the opening between Brains' nose and chin had widened. His mouth softened.

"Wait, I got one of her letters right in the drawer here—you can read it for yourself. Open it," Hitch invited, "so you won't think I'm trying to get out a rod. I'll stand here by the wall."

Brains reached past him, yanked at the drawer, looked down into it.

"Get it out," he said uncertainly, "show it to me, if you got it."

Hitch's hand had rested idly on the radio for a moment; the volume went up. "Just a song at twilight," it lisped. He fumbled hurriedly in the drawer, brought out an envelope, stripped it away with eager fingers. He unfolded the letter, turned it toward Brains, showed him the signature. "See? It's from her—'Goldie.'"

"Show me about the kid," said Brains gruffly.

Hitch turned it around, pointed to the bottom of the first page. "There it is, read it—I'll hold it up for you."

Brains had good eyes, he didn't have to come any closer. It stood out in black and white. *"I am taking good care of your baby for you. I think of you every time I look at it—"*

Hitch let the letter drop. His jaw wobbled. "Now go ahead, buddy, do like you said you were gonta," he sighed.

Brains' narrow stretch of brow was furrowed with uncertainty. He kept looking from the radio to the letter on the floor, and back to the radio again. "Still to us at twilight," it drooled, "comes love's old sweet song—" He blinked a couple of times. No moisture actually appeared in his eyes, but they had a faraway, gluey look. Hitch didn't seem to be breathing any more, he was so quiet.

There was a *clop* and the potato dropped off the downturned gun and split on the floor. Brains came to with an effort.

"And yuh named it after me?" he said. "Donleavy Hitchcock?"

The other nodded wistfully.

Brains took a deep breath. "I dunno," he said doubtfully, "maybe I'm wrong about letting ya get away with this; maybe I hadn't oughta—I never changed me mind before." He gave him a disgusted look. "Somehow ya got me outa the mood now—" He tucked the gun back under his arm, took possession of the room key on the bureau-top. "Go stand outside the door and wait there," he ordered curtly. "I ain't going out the front way, I'm leaving like I come in, see, without nobody being the wiser. You can tell 'em you locked yourself out. I don't want you in the room back of me while I'm crossing over."

Hitch was halfway through the door before he had finished speaking.

"And don't try nothing funny, or I may change me mind yet," Brains warned him. He thrust one leg through the window, found the plank, then turned his head to ask, "What color eyes has it got, anyway?" But Hitch hadn't waited to discuss the matter any further, he was far down the hall by that time, mopping his face on his sleeve as he ran.

Brains, dragging his feet after him across the plank like a cripple, muttered glumly, "How could I plug him when he named his kid after me? Maybe Fade was right. I oughta let up oncet in awhile. I guess I've bumped off enough guys. It won't hurt to let one off; maybe it'll bring me good luck."

It was easier going back than it had been coming over. The tilt of the board helped. He vaulted down over the low parapet onto the roof of the flat. He hauled the board over after him. Then he took Hitch's room key out of his pocket and calmly dropped it down the shaft; brushed his hands with a strange new feeling of nobility, of having done a good deed, that none of the actual killings he'd committed had ever been able to give him. He gave his hat a jaunty upward hoist in back, went in through the roof door, and started down the stairs to the street. He didn't care if anyone saw him or not now, but again no one did, just as when he'd come in.

He came out on the sidewalk and looked around for a taxi to take him back to Fade; he wanted his century back of course; he didn't need any alibi now. He hoped Fade wouldn't try to get petty-larceny about it, but he could show him his gun, fully loaded, to convince him he hadn't done it, if necessary. It wasn't exactly a taxi-using neighborhood; there weren't any in sight, so he started walking along, waiting to pick one up. He gave his hat another tilt from behind, he felt so good.

"Gee, it gives ya a funny feeling," he mumbled, "to have a kid named after ya."

By this time Hitch was back in his room again, having sent a bellboy in ahead of him with a passkey to make sure the coast was clear. He had the door closed, the window tightly latched, and the shade drawn, and just to be on the safe side he was checking out, going somewhere else to sleep, as soon as he could get his things together. But for the time being he was helpless, couldn't do a thing, just leaned there against the bureau shaking all over and with his head bobbing up and down. He wasn't shaking with fright, but with uncontrollable, splitting laughter. In his hand he held the letter from Brains' former ladylove, Goldie, that he'd picked up from the floor. At the bottom of the first page it said, just as Brains had read, *"taking good care of your baby. Think of you every time I look at it."* But every time he turned the page to the other side he went into a fresh spasm of hilarity. It went on: *"—and I'm sure glad you left it with me, never can tell what might turn up while you're gone. There's nothing like having a .32 around when a gal is by herself. Don't forget to pick up another in Chi for yourself, in case you run across you-know-who—"* The proud parent had to hold his sides, if he laughed any harder he was going to bust a rib.

Brains got a cab about three blocks down from the tenement. He didn't bother changing half-way, but out of consideration for Fade, he didn't ride straight up to the garage with it. He got out a short walk away from his destination. He could have gone back in the front way through "The Oasis" just as well as not now, but after all that trick out was Fade's bread-and-butter, so why spoil it for him? Why give it away to everyone at the bar?

They'd be bound to find out about it if he did that.

The garage entrance yawned as wide open as ever, but even the mechanic wasn't in sight this time; there didn't seem to be much business. He went in just like he'd come out, squeezing along between the wall and the line of parked cars, walking the bumper of the one that was pushed in too far, unseen by living eyes.

When he got a considerable distance past the open office door he could see the guy sitting in there, reading a paper. He circled around the wheelless chassis, found the slight ridge in the whitewashed wall that the out-thrust booth made, got a grip on it with his nails, eased the wedge out from under it, and got it open. He stayed in the booth until the wall had closed tight behind him, then looked out through the glass. The door to the front room was still closed, the door to Fade's office was still open waiting to welcome him. He stepped out of the booth, closed it behind him, sign and all, and then he stopped to listen. Gee, they were making a lot of noise out there—everyone's feet seemed to be running at once. Somebody was pounding on the door from the outside. They wanted Fade—he hadn't gotten back a minute too soon! He could hear the bartender hollering through, "Boss! Are ya'll right, boss? What's up, boss?" Brains twisted around and ducked into the office.

"I changed me mind," he gasped. "Just made it. They're callin' for ya—whadda they want out there? Wait'll I get my—!" His fingers went racing down the front of his topcoat, jacket; unbuttoning. He shrugged them both off his shoulders together and they slipped down his back. They caught at his elbows and stayed that way, half-on, half-off, while he blinked and stared across the table.

The set-up was the same—the cards, the drinks, the money—only Fade had dozed over it waiting for him to come back. His chin was down over his chest and his head kept going lower right while Brains was looking at him, sort of hitching a notch at a time. There was a funny bluish sort of haze in three horizontal lines hanging like a curtain right over Fade's head, and there wasn't any cigar around that he'd been smoking.,

Brains leaned across the table, gripped Fade by the shoulder, felt the warmth of his body through the shirt. "Hey, wake up—!" Then he saw the gun in Fade's lap where it had dropped, and the tag-end of the haze was still lazily coming from it. The chamois rag was down below on the floor. He knew the answer even before he'd picked up the gun, tilted Fade's face and looked at it. Fade had cleaned one of those guns of his once too often. When his head came up he only had one eye, it had gone right through the other.

The door out there slammed back and they came pouring through, everyone in the place. The room was suddenly choked with them. They saw him like that, straightening up across the desk, the gun in his hand, coat half-on. He felt somebody take the gun away from him, and then his arms were being held at his sides and the bartender was saying "What'd you do to him?" and sending out for cops. The hell with keeping his secret now, the guy was dead! He struggled violently, tried to free himself, couldn't.

"I just got in!" he roared. "He did it himself—I tell ya I just got in!"

"You been rowing with him all evening!" the bartender shouted. "Just a minute before the shot I heard him bawling you out; so did everyone else in the place—how can you say you just got in?"

Brains recoiled as though an invisible sledge-hammer had hit him, and slowly began to freeze where he stood. He could feel unidentified hands fumbling around him, cops' hands now, and kept trying to think his way out; kept trying to think while they compared the I.O.U. he'd taken back from Fade with the new one he'd given him afterwards. He shook his head as if he was groggy, trying to clear it.

"Wait, lemme show you," he heard himself saying, "there's a dummy telephone-booth right outside the door there; I came in through it right after it happened—lemme show you!"

He knew they'd let him all right, knew they'd go and look at it—but somehow he already knew what good it was going to do him. No one had seen him go and no one had seen him come. Only Hitch, and just try to get Hitch to help him!

As he led them outside toward it, body straining downward toward the floor in his eagerness to get there quick, he kept whimpering under his breath, "Six guys I killed and they never touch me for it; the seventh I let live, and they hook me for a killing I never even done at all!"

MOMENTUM

PAINE HUNG AROUND OUTSIDE the house waiting for old Ben Burroughs' caller to go, because he wanted to see him alone. You can't very well ask anyone for a loan of $250 in the presence of someone else, especially when you have a pretty strong hunch you're going to be turned down flat and told where to get off, into the bargain.

But he had a stronger reason for not wanting witnesses to his interview with the old skinflint. The large handkerchief in his back pocket, folded triangularly, had a special purpose, and that little instrument in another pocket —wasn't it to be used in prying open a window?

While he lurked in the shrubbery, watching the lighted window and Burroughs' seated form inside it, he kept rehearsing the plea he'd composed, as though he were still going to use it.

"Mr. Burroughs, I know it's late, and I know you'd rather not be reminded that I exist, but desperation can't wait; and I'm desperate." That sounded good. "Mr. Burroughs, I worked for your concern faithfully for ten long years, and the last six months of its existence, to help keep it going. I voluntarily worked at half-wages, on your given word that my defaulted pay would be made up as soon as things got better. Instead of that, you went into phony bankruptcy to cancel your obligations."

Then a little soft soap to take the sting out of it. "I haven't come near you all these years, and I haven't come to make trouble now. If I thought you really didn't have the money, I still wouldn't. But it's common knowledge by now that the bankruptcy was feigned; it's obvious by the way you continue to live that you salvaged your own investment; and I've lately heard rumors of your backing a dummy corporation under another name to take up where you left off. Mr. Burroughs, the exact amount of the six months' promissory half-wages due me is two hundred and fifty dollars."

Just the right amount of dignity and self-respect, Pauline had commented at this point; not wishy-washy or maudlin, just quiet and effective.

And then for a bang-up finish, and every word of it true. "Mr. Burroughs, I have to have help tonight; it can't wait another twenty-four hours. There's a hole the size of a fifty-cent piece in the sole of each of my shoes, I have a wedge of cardboard in the bottom of each one. We haven't had light or gas in a week now. There's a bailiff coming tomorrow morning to put out the little that's left of our furniture and seal the door.

"If I was alone in this, I'd still fight it through, without going to anyone. But, Mr. Burroughs, I have a wife at home to support. You may not remember her, a pretty little dark-haired girl who once worked as a stenographer in your office for a month or two. You surely wouldn't know her now, she's aged twenty years in the past two."

That was about all. That was about all anyone could have said. And yet Paine knew he was licked before he even uttered a word of it.

He couldn't see the old man's visitor. The caller was out of range of the window. Burroughs was seated in a line with it, profile toward Paine. Paine could see his mean, thin-lipped mouth moving. Once or twice he raised his hand in a desultory gesture. Then he seemed to be listening and finally he nodded slowly. He held his forefinger up and shook it, as if impressing some point on his auditor. After that he rose and moved deeper into the room, but without getting out of line with the window.

He stood against the far wall, hand out to a tapestry hanging there. Paine craned his neck, strained his eyes. There must be a wall safe behind there the old codger was about to open.

If he only had a pair of binoculars handy.

Paine saw the old miser pause, turn his head and make some request of the other person. A hand abruptly grasped the looped shade cord and drew the shade to the bottom.

Paine gritted his teeth. The old fossil wasn't taking any chances, was he? You'd think he was a mind-reader, knew there was someone out there. But a chink remained, slowing a line of light at the bottom. Paine sidled out of his hiding place and slipped up to the window. He put his eyes to it, focused on Burroughs' dialing hand, to the exclusion of everything else.

A three-quarters turn to the left, about to where the numeral 8 would be on the face of the clock. Then back to about where 3 would be. Then back the other way, this time to 10. Simple enough. He must remember that—8–3–10.

Burroughs was opening it now and bringing out a cash box. He set it down on the table and opened it. Paine's eyes hardened and his mouth twisted sullenly. Look at all that money! The old fossil's gnarled hand dipped into it, brought out a sheaf of bills, counted them. He put back a few, counted the remainder a second time and set them on the table top while he returned the cash box, closed the safe, straightened out the tapestry.

A blurred figure moved partly into the way at this point, too close to the shade gap to come clearly into focus; but without obliterating the little stack of bills on the table. Burroughs' claw-like hand picked them up, held them out. A second hand, smoother, reached for them. The two hands shook.

Paine prudently retreated to his former lookout point. He knew where the safe was now, that was all that mattered. He wasn't a moment too soon. The shade shot up an instant later, this time with Burroughs' hand guiding its cord. The other person had withdrawn offside again. Burroughs moved after him out of range, and the room abruptly darkened. A moment later a light flickered on in the porch ceiling.

Paine quickly shifted to the side of the house, in the moment's grace given him, in order to make sure his presence wasn't detected.

The door opened. Burroughs' voice croaked a curt "Night," to which the departing visitor made no answer. The interview had evidently not been an altogether cordial one. The door closed again, with quite a little force. A quick step crossed the porch, went along the cement walk to the street, away from where Paine stood pressed flat against the side of the house. He didn't bother trying to see who it was. It was too dark for that, and his primary purpose was to keep his own presence concealed.

When the anonymous tread had safely died away in the distance, Paine moved to where he could command the front of the house. Burroughs was alone in it now, he knew; he was too niggardly even to employ a full-time servant. A dim light showed for a moment or two through the fanlight over the door, coming from the back of the hall. Now was the time to ring the doorbell, if he expected to make his plea to the old duffer before he retired.

He knew that, and yet something seemed to be keeping him from stepping up onto the porch and ringing the doorbell. He knew what it was, too, but he wouldn't admit it to himself.

"He'll only say no point-blank and slam the door in

my face" was the excuse he gave himself as he crouched back in the shrubbery, waiting. "And then once he's seen me out here, I'll be the first one he'll suspect afterwards when—"

The fanlight had gone dark now and Burroughs was on his way upstairs. A bedroom window on the floor above lighted up. There was still time; if he rang even now, Burroughs would come downstairs again and answer the door. But Paine didn't make the move, stayed there patiently waiting.

The bedroom window blacked out at last, and the house was now dark and lifeless. Paine stayed there, still fighting with himself. Not a battle, really, because that had been lost long ago; but still giving himself excuses for what he knew he was about to do. Excuses for not going off about his business and remaining what he had been until now—an honest man.

How could he face his wife, if he came back empty-handed tonight? Tomorrow their furniture would be piled on the sidewalk. Night after night he had promised to tackle Burroughs, and each time he'd put it off, walked past the house without summoning up nerve enough to go through with it. Why? For one thing, he didn't have the courage to stomach the sharp-tongued, sneering refusal that he was sure he'd get. But the more important thing had been the realization that once he made his plea, he automatically canceled this other, unlawful way of getting the money. Burroughs had probably forgotten his existence after all these years, but if he reminded him of it by interviewing him ahead of time—

He tightened his belt decisively. Well, he wasn't coming home to her empty-handed tonight, but he still wasn't going to tackle Burroughs for it either. She'd never need to find out just how he'd got it.

He straightened and looked all around him. No one in sight. The house was isolated. Most of the streets around it were only laid out and paved by courtesy; they bordered vacant lots. He moved in cautiously but determinedly toward the window of that room where he had seen the safe.

Cowardice can result in the taking of more risks than the most reckless courage. He was afraid of little things —afraid of going home and facing his wife empty-handed, afraid of asking an ill-tempered old reprobate for money because he knew he would be reviled and driven away—and so he was about to break into a house, become a burglar for the first time in his life.

It opened so easily. It was almost an invitation to unlawful entry. He stood up on the sill, and the cover of a paper book of matches, thrust into the intersection between the two window halves, pushed the tongue of the latch out of the way.

He dropped down to the ground, applied the little instrument he had brought to the lower frame, and it slid effortlessly up. A minute later he was in the room, had closed the window so it wouldn't look suspicious from the outside. He wondered why he'd always thought until now it took skill and patience to break into a house. There was nothing to it.

He took out the folded handkerchief and tied it around the lower part of his face. For a minute he wasn't going to bother with it, and later he was sorry he had, in one way. And then again, it probably would have happened anyway, even without it. It wouldn't keep him from being seen, only from being identified.

He knew enough not to light the room lights, but he had nothing so scientific as a pocket torch with him to take their place. He had to rely on ordinary matches, which meant he could only use one hand for the safe dial, after he had cleared the tapestry out of the way.

It was a toy thing, a gimcrack. He hadn't even the exact combination, just the approximate position—8–3–10. It wouldn't work the first time, so he varied it slightly, and then it clicked free.

He opened it, brought out the cash box, set it on the table. It was as though the act of setting it down threw a master electric switch. The room was suddenly drenched with light and Burroughs stood in the open doorway, bathrobe around his weazened frame, left hand out to the wall switch, right hand holding a gun trained on Paine.

Paine's knees knocked together, his windpipe constricted, and he died a little—the way only an amateur caught red-handed at his first attempt can, a professional never. His thumb stung unexpectedly, and he mechanically whipped out the live match he was holding.

"Just got down in time, didn't I?" the old man said with spiteful satisfaction. "It mayn't be much of a safe, but it sets off a buzzer up by my bed every time it swings open—see?"

He should have moved straight across to the phone, right there in the room with Paine, and called for help, but he had a vindictive streak in him, he couldn't resist standing and rubbing it in.

"Ye know what ye're going to get for this, don't ye?" he went on, licking his indrawn lips. "And I'll see that ye get it too, every last month of it that's coming to ye." He took a step forward. "Now get away from that. Get all the way back over there and don't ye make a move until I—"

A sudden dawning suspicion entered his glittering little eyes. "Wait a minute. Haven't I seen you somewhere before? There's something familiar about you." He moved closer. "Take off that mask," he ordered. "Let me see who the devil you are!"

Paine became panic-stricken at the thought of revealing his face. He didn't stop to think that as long as Burroughs had him at gun point anyway, and he couldn't get away, the old man was bound to find out who he was sooner or later.

He shook his head in unreasoning terror.

"No!" he panted hoarsely, billowing out the handkerchief over his mouth. He even tried to back away, but there was a chair or something in the way, and he couldn't.

That brought the old man in closer. "Then by golly I'll take it off for ye!" he snapped. He reached out for the lower triangular point of it. His right hand slanted out of line with Paine's body as he did so, was no longer exactly covering it with the gun. But the variation was nothing to take a chance on.

Cowardice. Cowardice that spurs you to a rashness the stoutest courage would quail from. Paine didn't stop to think of the gun. He suddenly hooked onto both the old man's arms, spread-eagled them. It was such a harebrained chance to take that Burroughs wasn't expecting it, and accordingly it worked. The gun clicked futilely, pointed up toward the ceiling; it must have jammed, or else the first chamber was empty and Burroughs hadn't known it.

Paine kept warding that arm off at a wide angle. But his chief concern was the empty hand clawing toward the handkerchief. That he swiveled far downward the other way, out of reach. He twisted the scrawny skin around the old man's skinny right wrist until pain made the hand flop over open and drop the gun. It fell between them to the floor, and Paine scuffed it a foot or two out of reach with the side of his foot.

Then he locked that same foot behind one of Burroughs' and pushed him over it. The old man went sprawling backwards on the floor, and the short, unequal struggle was over. Yet even as he went, he was victorious. His downflung left arm, as Paine released it to send him over, swept up in an arc, clawed, and took the handkerchief with it.

He sprawled there now, cradled on the point of one elbow, breathing malign recognition that was like a knife through Paine's heart. "You're Dick Paine, you dirty crook! I know ye now! You're Dick Paine, my old employee! You're going to pay for this—"

That was all he had time to say. That was his own death warrant. Paine was acting under such neuro-muscular compulsion, brought on by the instinct of self-preservation, that he wasn't even conscious of stooping to retrieve the fallen gun. The next thing he knew it was in his hand, pointed toward the accusing mouth that was all he was afraid of.

He jerked the trigger. For the second time it clicked— either jammed or unloaded at that chamber. He was to have that on his conscience afterwards, that click—like a last chance given him to keep from doing what he was about to do. That made it something different, that took away the shadowy little excuse he would have had until now; that changed it from an impulsive act committed in the heat of combat to a deed of cold-blooded, deliberate murder, with plenty of time to think twice before it was committed. And conscience makes cowards of us all. And he was a coward to begin with.

Burroughs even had time to sputter the opening sylla-bles of a desperate plea for mercy, a promise of immu-nity. True, he probably wouldn't have kept it.

"Don't! Paine—Dick, don't! I won't say anything. I won't tell 'em you were here—"

But Burroughs knew who he was. Paine tugged at the trigger, and the third chamber held death in it. This time the gun crashed, and Burroughs' whole face was veiled in a huff of smoke. By the time it had thinned he was already dead, head on the floor, a tenuous thread of red streaking from the corner of his mouth, as though he had no more than split his lip.

Paine was the amateur even to the bitter end. In the death hush that followed, his first half-audible remark was: "Mr. Burroughs, I didn't mean to—"

Then he just stared in white-faced consternation.

"Now I've done it! I've killed a man—and they kill you for that! Now I'm in for it!"

He looked at the gun, appalled, as though it alone, and not he, was to blame for what had happened. He picked up the handkerchief, dazedly rubbed at the weapon, then desisted again. It seemed to him safer to take it with him, even though it was Burroughs' own. He had an amateur's mystic dread of fingerprints. He was sure he wouldn't be able to clean it thoroughly enough to remove all traces of his own handling; even in the very act of trying to clean it, he might leave others. He sheathed it in the inner pocket of his coat.

He looked this way and that. He'd better get out of here; he'd better get out of here. Already the drums of flight were beginning to beat in him, and he knew they'd never be silent again.

The cash box was still standing there on the table where he'd left it, and he went to it, flung the lid up. He didn't want this money any more, it had curdled for him, it had become bloody money. But he had to have some, at least; to make it easier to keep from getting caught. He didn't stop to count how much there was in it; there must have been at least a thousand, by the looks of it. Maybe even fifteen or eighteen hundred.

He wouldn't take a cent more than was coming to him. He'd only take the two hundred and fifty he'd come here to get. To his frightened mind that seemed to make his crime less heinous, if he contented himself with taking just what was rightfully his. That seemed to keep it from being outright murder and robbery, enabled him to maintain the fiction that it had been just a collection of a debt accompanied by a frightful and unforeseen accident. And one's conscience, after all, is the most dreaded policeman of the lot.

And furthermore, he realized as he hastily counted it out, thrust the sum into his back trouser pocket, but-

toned the pocket down, he couldn't tell his wife that he'd
been here—or she'd know what he'd done. He'd have to
make her think that he'd got the money somewhere else.
That shouldn't be hard. He'd put off coming here to see
Burroughs night after night, he'd shown her plainly that
he hadn't relished the idea of approaching his former
boss; she'd been the one who had kept egging him on.

Only tonight she'd said, "I don't think you'll ever carry
it out. I've about given up hope."

So what more natural than to let her think that in the
end he hadn't? He'd think up some other explanation to
account for the presence of the money; he'd have to. If
not right tonight, then tomorrow. It would come to him
after the shock of this had worn off a little and he could
think more calmly.

Had he left anything around that would betray him,
that they could trace to him? He'd better put the cash
box back; there was just a chance that they wouldn't
know exactly how much the old skinflint had had on
hand. They often didn't, with his type. He wiped it off
carefully with the handkerchief he'd had around his face,
twisted the dial closed on it, dabbed at that. He didn't go
near the window again; he put out the light and made his
way out by the front door of the house.

He opened it with the handkerchief and closed it after
him again, and after an exhaustive survey of the desolate
street, came down off the porch, moved quickly along
the front walk, turned left along the gray tape of sidewalk that threaded the gloom, toward the distant trolley
line that he wasn't going to board at this particular stop,
at this particular hour.

He looked up once or twice at the star-flecked sky as
he trudged along. It was over. That was all there was to
it. Just a jealously guarded secret now. A memory, that
he daren't share with anyone else, not even Pauline. But
deep within him he knew better. It wasn't over, it was
just beginning. That had been just the curtain raiser,

back there. Murder, like a snowball rolling down a
slope, gathers momentum as it goes.

He had to have a drink. He had to try to drown the
damn thing out of him. He couldn't go home dry with it
on his mind. They stayed open until four, didn't they,
places like that? He wasn't much of a drinker, he wasn't
familiar with details like that. Yes, there was one over
there, on the other side of the street. And this was far
enough away, more than two-thirds of the way from
Burroughs' to his own place.

It was empty. That might be better; then again it might
not. He could be too easily remembered. Well, too late
now, he was already at the bar. "A straight whiskey."
The barman didn't even have time to turn away before
he spoke again. "Another one."

He shouldn't have done that; that looked suspicious,
to gulp it that quick.

"Turn that radio off," he said hurriedly. He shouldn't
have said that, that sounded suspicious. The barman had
looked at him when he did. And the silence was worse, if
anything. Unbearable. Those throbbing drums of danger. "Never mind, turn it on again."

"Make up your mind, mister," the barman said in mild
reproof.

He seemed to be doing all the wrong things. He
shouldn't have come in here at all, to begin with. Well,
he'd get out, before he put his foot in it any worse. "How
much?" He took out the half-dollar and the quarter that
was all he had.

"Eighty cents."

His stomach dropped an inch. Not *that* money! He
didn't want to have to bring that out, it would show too
plainly on his face. "Most places they charge thirty-five a
drink."

"Not this brand. You didn't specify." But the barman
was on guard now, scenting a dead beat. He was leaning
over the counter, right square in front of him, in a posi-

tion to take in every move he made with his hands.

He shouldn't have ordered that second drink. Just for a nickel he was going to have to take that whole wad out right under this man's eyes. And maybe he wouldn't remember that tomorrow, after the jumpy way Paine had acted in here!

"Where's the washroom?"

"That door right back there behind the cigarette machine." But the barman was now plainly suspicious; Paine could tell that by the way he kept looking at him.

Paine closed it after him, sealed it with his shoulder-blades, unbuttoned his back pocket, riffled through the money, looking for the smallest possible denomination. A ten was the smallest, and there was only one of them; that would have to do. He cursed himself for getting into such a spot.

The door suddenly gave a heave behind him. Not a violent one, but he wasn't expecting it. It threw him forward off balance. The imperfectly grasped outspread fan of money in his hand went scattering all over the floor. The barman's head showed through the aperture. He started to say: "I don't like the way you're acting. Come on now, get out of my pla—" Then he saw the money.

Burroughs' gun had been an awkward bulk for his inside coat pocket all along. The grip was too big, it overspanned the lining. His abrupt lurch forward had shifted it. It felt as if it was about to fall out of its own weight. He clutched at it to keep it in.

The barman saw the gesture, closed in on him with a grunted "I thought so!" that might have meant nothing or everything.

He was no Burroughs to handle, he was an ox of a man. He pinned Paine back against the wall and held him there more or less helpless. Even so, if he'd only shut up, it probably wouldn't have happened. But he made a tunnel of his mouth and bayed: "Pol-eece! Holdup! Help!"

Paine lost the little presence of mind he had left, became a blurred pinwheel of hand motion, impossible to control or forestall. Something exploded against the barman's midriff, as though he'd had a firecracker tucked in under his belt.

He coughed his way down to the floor and out of the world.

Another one. Two now. Two in less than an hour. Paine didn't think the words, they seemed to glow out at him, emblazoned on the grimy washroom walls in characters of fire, like in that Biblical story.

He took a step across the prone, white-aproned form as stiffly as though he were high up on stilts. He looked out through the door crack. No one in the bar. And it probably hadn't been heard outside in the street; it had had two doors to go through.

He put the damned thing away, the thing that seemed to be spreading death around just by being in his possession. If he hadn't brought it with him from Burroughs' house, this man would have been alive now. But if he hadn't brought it with him, he would have been apprehended for the first murder by now. Why blame the weapon, why not just blame fate?

That money, all over the floor. He squatted, went for it bill by bill, counting it as he went. Twenty, forty, sixty, eighty. Some of them were on one side of the corpse, some on the other; he had to cross over, not once but several times, in the course of his grisly paper chase. One was even pinned partly under him, and when he'd wangled it out, there was a swirl of blood on the edge. He grimaced, thrust it out, blotted it off. Some of it stayed on, of course.

He had it all now, or thought he did. He couldn't stay in here another minute, he felt as if he were choking. He got it all into his pocket any old way, buttoned it down.

Then he eased out, this time looking behind him at what he'd done, not before him. That was how he missed seeing the drunk, until it was too late and the drunk had already seen him.

The drunk was pretty drunk, but maybe not drunk enough to take a chance on. He must have weaved in quietly, while Paine was absorbed in retrieving the money. He was bending over reading the list of selections on the coin phonograph. He raised his head before Paine could get back in again, and to keep him from seeing what lay on the floor in there Paine quickly closed the door behind him.

"Say, itsh about time," the drunk complained. "How about a little servish here?"

Paine tried to shadow his face as much as he could with the brim of his hat. "I'm not in charge here," he mumbled, "I'm just a customer myself—"

The drunk was going to be sticky. He barnacled onto Paine's lapels as he tried to sidle by. "Don't gimme that. You just hung up your coat in there, you think you're quitting for the night. Well you ain't quitting until I've had my drink—"

Paine tried to shake him off without being too violent about it and bringing on another hand-to-hand set-to. He hung on like grim death. Or rather, he hung on to grim death—without knowing it.

Paine fought down the flux of panic, the ultimate result of which he'd already seen twice now. Any minute someone might come in from the street. Someone sober. "All right," he breathed heavily, "hurry up, what'll it be?"

"Thass more like it, now you're being reg'lar guy." The drunk released him and he went around behind the bar. "Never anything but good ole Four Roses for mine truly—"

Paine snatched down a bottle at random from the shelf, handed it over bodily. "Here, help yourself. You'll have to take it outside with you, I'm—we're closing up for the night now." He found a switch, threw it. It only made part of the lights go out. There was no time to bother with the rest. He hustled the bottle-nursing drunk out ahead of him, pulled the door to after the two of them, so that it would appear to be locked even if it wasn't.

The drunk started to make loud plaint, looping around on the sidewalk. "You're a fine guy, not even a glass to drink it out of!"

Paine gave him a slight push in one direction, wheeled and made off in the other.

The thing was, how drunk was he? Would he remember Paine, would he know him if he saw him again? He hurried on, spurred to a run by the night-filling hails and imprecations resounding behind him. He couldn't do it again. Three lives in an hour. He couldn't!

The night was fading when he turned into the little courtyard that was his own. He staggered up the stairs, but not from the two drinks he'd had, from the two deaths.

He stood outside his own door at last—3-B. It seemed such a funny thing to do after killing people—fumble around in your pockets for your latchkey and fit it in, just like other nights. He'd been an honest man when he'd left here, and now he'd come back a murderer. A double one.

He hoped she was asleep. He couldn't face her right now, couldn't talk to her even if he tried. He was all in emotionally. She'd find out right away just by looking at his face, by looking in his eyes.

He eased the front door closed, tiptoed to the bedroom, looked in. She was lying there asleep. Poor thing, poor helpless thing, married to a murderer.

He went back, undressed in the outer room. Then he stayed in there. Not even stretched out on top of the sofa, but crouched beside it on the floor, head and arms pillowed against its seat. The drums of terror kept pounding. They kept saying, "What am I gonna do now?"

The sun seemed to shoot up in the sky, it got to the top so fast. He opened his eyes and it was all the way up. He went to the door and brought in the paper. It wasn't in the morning papers yet, they were made up too soon after midnight.

He turned around and Pauline had come out, was picking up his things. "All over the floor, never saw a man like you—"

He said, "Don't—" and stabbed his hand toward her, but it was already too late. He'd jammed the bills in so haphazardly the second time, in the bar, that they made a noticeable bulge there in his back pocket. She opened it and took them out, and some of them dribbled onto the floor.

She just stared. "Dick!" She was incredulous, overjoyed. "Not Burroughs? Don't tell me you finally—"

"No!" The name went through him like a red-hot skewer. "I didn't go anywhere near him. He had nothing to do with it!"

She nodded corroboratively. "I thought not, because—"

He wouldn't let her finish. He stepped close to her, took her by both shoulders. "Don't mention his name to me again. I don't want to hear his name again. I got it from someone else."

"Who?"

He knew he'd have to answer her, or she'd suspect something. He swallowed, groped blindly for a name. "Charlie Chalmers," he blurted out.

"But he refused you only last week!"

"Well, he changed his mind." He turned on her tormentedly. "Don't ask me any more questions, Pauline, I can't stand it! I haven't slept all night. There it is, that's all that matters." He took his trousers from her, went into the bathroom to dress. He'd hidden Burroughs' gun the night before in the built-in laundry hamper in there; he wished he'd hidden the money with it. He put the gun back in the pocket where he'd carried it last night. If she touched him there—

He combed his hair. The drums were a little quieter now, but he knew they'd come back again; this was just the lull before the storm.

He came out again, and she was putting cups on the table. She looked worried now. She sensed that something was wrong. She was afraid to ask him, he could see, maybe afraid of what she'd find out. He couldn't sit here eating, just as though this was any other day. Any minute someone might come here after him.

He passed by the window. Suddenly he stiffened, gripped the curtain. "What's that man doing down there?" She came up behind him. "Standing there talking to the janitor—"

"Why, Dick, what harm is there in that? A dozen people a day stop and chat with—"

He edged back a step behind the frame. "He's looking up at our windows! Did you see that? They both turned and looked up this way! Get back!" His arm swept her around behind him.

"Why should we? We haven't done anything."

"They're coming in the entrance to this wing! They're on their way up here—"

"Dick, why are you acting this way, what's happened?"

"Go in the bedroom and wait there." He was a coward, yes. But there are varieties. At least he wasn't a coward that hid behind a woman's skirts. He prodded her in there ahead of him. Then he gripped her shoulder a minute. "Don't ask any questions. If you love me, stay in here until they go away again."

He closed the door on her frightened face. He cracked the gun. Two left in it. "I can get them both," he thought, "if I'm careful. I've got to."

It was going to happen again.

The jangle of the doorbell battery steeled him. He moved with deadly slowness toward the door, feet flat and firm upon the floor. He picked up the newspaper from the table on his way by, rolled it into a funnel, thrust his hand and the gun down into it. The pressure of his arm against his side was sufficient to keep it furled. It was as though he had just been reading and had carelessly tucked the paper under his arm. It hid the gun effectively as long as he kept it slanting down.

He freed the latch and shifted slowly back with the door, bisected by its edge, the unarmed half of him all that showed. The janitor came into view first, as the gap widened. He was on the outside. The man next to him had a derby hat riding the back of his head, a bristly mustache, was rotating a cigar between his teeth. He looked like—one of those who come after you.

The janitor said with scarcely veiled insolence, "Paine, I've got a man here looking for a flat. I'm going to show him yours, seeing as how it'll be available from today on. Any objections?"

Paine swayed there limply against the door like a garment bag hanging on a hook, as they brushed by. "No," he whispered deflatedly. "No, go right ahead."

He held the door open to make sure their descent continued all the way down to the bottom. As soon as he'd closed it, Pauline caught him anxiously by the arm. "Why wouldn't you let me tell them we're able to pay the arrears now and are staying? Why did you squeeze my arm like that?"

"Because we're not staying, and I don't want them to know we've got the money. I don't want anyone to know. We're getting out of here."

"Dick, what is it? Have you done something you shouldn't?"

"Don't ask me. Listen, if you love me, don't ask any questions. I'm—in a little trouble. I've got to get out of here. Never mind why. If you don't want to come with me, I'll go alone."

"Anywhere you go, I'll go." Her eyes misted. "But can't it be straightened out?"

Two men dead beyond recall. He gave a bitter smile. "No, it can't."

"Is it bad?"

He shut his eyes, took a minute to answer. "It's bad, Pauline. That's all you need to know. That's all I want you to know. I've got to get out of here as fast as I can. From one minute to the next it may be too late. Let's get started now. They'll be here to dispossess us sometime today anyway, that'll be a good excuse. We won't wait, we'll leave now."

She went in to get ready. She took so long doing it he nearly went crazy. She didn't seem to realize how urgent it was. She wasted as much time deciding what to take and what to leave behind as though they were going on a weekend jaunt to the country. He kept going to the bedroom door, urging, "Pauline, hurry! Faster, Pauline!"

She cried a great deal. She was an obedient wife; she didn't ask him any more questions about what the trouble was. She just cried about it without knowing what it was.

He was down on hands and knees beside the window, in the position of a man looking for a collar button under a dresser, when she finally came out with the small bag she'd packed. He turned a stricken face to her. "Too late—I can't leave with you. Someone's already watching the place."

She inclined herself to his level, edged up beside him. "Look straight over to the other side of the street. See him? He hasn't moved for the past ten minutes. People don't just stand like that for no reason—"

"He may be waiting for someone."

"He is," he murmured somberly. "Me."

"But you can't be sure."

"No, but if I put it to the test by showing myself, it'll be too late by the time I find out. You go by yourself, ahead of me."

"No, if you stay, let me stay with you—"

"I'm not staying, I can't! I'll follow you and meet you somewhere. But it'll be easier for us to leave one at a time than both together. I can slip over the roof or go out the basement way. He won't stop you, they're not looking for you. You go now and wait for me. No, I have a better idea. Here's what you do. You get two tickets and get on the train at the downtown terminal without waiting for me—" He was separating some of the money, thrusting it into her reluctant hand while he spoke. "Now listen closely. Two tickets to Montreal—"

An added flicker of dismay showed in her eyes. "We're leaving the country?"

When you've committed murder, you have no country any more. "We have to, Pauline. Now there's an eight o'clock limited for there every night. It leaves the downtown terminal at eight sharp. It stops for five minutes at the station uptown at twenty after. That's where I'll get on. Make sure you're on it or we'll miss each other. Keep a seat for me next to you in the day coach—"

She clung to him despairingly. "No, no. I'm afraid you won't come. Something'll happen. You'll miss it. If I leave you now I may never see you again. I'll find myself making the trip up there alone, without you—"

He tried to reassure her, pressing her hands between his. "Pauline, I give you my word of honor—" That was no good, he was a murderer now. "Pauline, I swear to you—"

"Here—on this. Take a solemn oath on this, otherwise

I won't go." She took out a small carnelian cross she carried in her handbag, attached to a little gold chain— one of the few things they hadn't pawned. She palmed it, pressed the flat of his right hand over it. They looked into each other's eyes with sacramental intensity.

His voice trembled. "I swear nothing will keep me from that train; I'll join you on it no matter what happens, no matter who tries to stop me. Rain or shine, *dead or alive*, I'll meet you aboard it at eight-twenty tonight!"

She put it away, their lips brushed briefly but fervently.

"Hurry up now," he urged. "He's still there. Don't look at him on your way past. If he should stop you and ask who you are, give another name—"

He went to the outside door with her, watched her start down the stairs. The last thing she whispered up was: "Dick, be careful for my sake. Don't let anything happen to you between now and tonight."

He went back to the window, crouched down, cheek-bones to sill. She came out under him in a minute or two. She knew enough not to look up at their windows, although the impulse must have been strong. The man was still standing over there. He didn't seem to notice her. He even looked off in another direction.

She passed from view behind the building line; their windows were set in on the court that indented it. Paine wondered if he'd ever see her again. Sure he would, he had to. He realized that it would be better for her if he didn't. It wasn't fair to enmesh her in his own doom. But he'd sworn an oath, and he meant to keep it.

Two, three minutes ticked by. The cat-and-mouse play continued. He crouched motionless by the window, the other man stood motionless across the street. She must be all the way down at the corner by now. She'd take the bus there, to go downtown. She might have to wait a few minutes for one to come along, she might still be in sight.

But if the man was going to go after her, accost her, he would have started by now. He wouldn't keep standing there.

Then, as Paine watched, he did start. He looked down that way, threw away something he'd been smoking, began to move purposefully in that direction. There was no mistaking the fact that he was looking *at* or *after* someone, by the intent way he held his head. He passed from sight.

Paine began to breathe hot and fast. "I'll kill him. If he touches her, tries to stop her, I'll kill him right out in the open street in broad daylight." It was still fear, coward-ice, that was at work, although it was almost unrecogniz-able as such by now.

He felt for the gun, left his hand on it, inside the breast of his coat, straightened to his feet, ran out of the flat and down the stairs. He cut across the little set-in paved courtyard at a sprint, flashed out past the sheltering building line, turned down in the direction they had both taken.

Then as the panorama before him registered, he stag-gered to an abrupt stop, stood taking it in. It offered three component but separate points of interest. He only noticed two at first. One was the bus down at the corner. The front-third of it protruded, door open. He caught a glimpse of Pauline's back as she was in the act of step-ping in, unaccompanied and unmolested.

The door closed automatically, and it swept across the vista and disappeared at the other side. On the other side of the street, but nearer at hand, the man who had been keeping the long vigil had stopped a second time, was gesticulating angrily to a woman laden with parcels whom he had joined. Both voices were so raised they reached Paine without any trouble.

"A solid half-hour I've been standing there and no one home to let me in!"

"Well, is it my fault you went off without your key? Next time take it with you!"

Nearer at hand still, on Paine's own side of the street, a lounging figure detached itself from the building wall and impinged on his line of vision. The man had been only yards away the whole time, but Paine's eyes had been trained on the distance, he'd failed to notice him until now.

His face suddenly loomed out at Paine. His eyes bored into Paine's with unmistakable intent. He didn't look like one of those that come to get you. He acted like it. He thumbed his vest pocket for something, some credential or identification. He said in a soft, slurring voice that held an inflexible command in it, "Just a minute there, buddy. Your name's Paine, ain't it? I want to see you—"

Paine didn't have to give his muscular coordination any signal; it acted for him automatically. He felt his legs carry him back into the shelter of the courtyard in a sort of slithering jump. He was in at the foot of the public stairs before the other man had even rounded the building line. He was in behind his own door before the remorselessly slow but plainly audible tread had started up them.

The man seemed to be coming up after him alone. Didn't he know Paine had a gun? He'd find out. He was up on the landing now. He seemed to know which floor to stop at, which door to come to a halt before. Probably the janitor had told him. Then why hadn't he come sooner? Maybe he'd been waiting for someone to join him, and Paine had upset the plan by showing himself so soon.

Paine realized he'd trapped himself by returning here. He should have gone on up to the roof and over. But the natural instinct of the hunted, whether four-legged or two, is to find a hole, get in out of the open. It was too late now: he was right out there on the other side of the door. Paine tried to keep his harried breathing silent.

To his own ears it grated like sand sifted through a sieve.

He didn't ring the bell and he didn't knock; he tried the knob, in a half-furtive, half-badgering way. That swirl of panic began to churn in Paine again. He couldn't let him get in; he couldn't let him get away, either. He'd only go and bring others back with him.

Paine pointed the muzzle of the gun to the crack of the door, midway between the two hinges. With his other hand he reached out for the catch that controlled the latch, released it.

Now if he wanted to die, he should open this door.

The man had kept on trying the knob. Now the door slipped in past the frame. The crack at the other side widened in accompaniment as it swung around. Paine ran the gun bore up it even with the side of his head.

The crash was thunderous. He fell into the flat, with only his feet and ankles outside.

Paine came out from behind the door, dragged him the rest of the way in, closed it. He stopped, his hands probed here and there. He found a gun, a heftier, more businesslike one than his. He took that. He found a billfold heavy with cash. He took that, too. He fished for the badge.

There wasn't any in the vest pocket he'd seen him reach toward downstairs. There was only a block of cheaply printed cards. *Star Finance Company. Loans. Up to any amount without security.*

So he hadn't been one, after all; he'd evidently been some kind of a loan shark, drawn by the scent of Paine's difficulties.

Three times now in less than twenty-four hours.

Instinctively he knew he was doomed now, if he hadn't before. There wasn't any more of the consternation he had felt the first two times. He kept buying off time with bullets, that was all it was now. And the rate of interest kept going higher, the time limit kept shortening. There wasn't even any time to feel sorry.

Doors had begun opening outside in the hall, voices were calling back and forth. "What was that—a shot?"

"It sounded like in 3-B."

He'd have to get out now, right away, or he'd be trapped in here again. And this time for good. He shifted the body out of the line of vision from outside, buttoned up his jacket, took a deep breath; then he opened the door, stepped out, closed it after him. Each of the other doors was open with someone peering out from it. They hadn't ganged up yet in the middle of the hall. Most of them were women, anyway. One or two edged timidly back when they saw him emerge.

"It wasn't anything," he said. "I dropped a big clay jug in there just now."

He knew they didn't believe him.

He started down the stairs. At the third step he looked over the side, saw the cop coming up. Somebody had already phoned or sent out word. He reversed, flashed around his own landing, and on up from there.

The cop's voice said, "Stop where you are!" He was coming on fast now. But Paine was going just as fast.

The cop's voice said, "Get inside, all of you! I'm going to shoot!"

Doors began slapping shut like firecrackers. Paine switched over abruptly to the rail and shot first.

The cop jolted, but he grabbed the rail and stayed up. He didn't die as easy as the others. He fired four times before he lost his gun. He missed three times and hit Paine the fourth time.

It went in his chest on the right side, and knocked him across the width of the staircase. It flamed with pain, and then it didn't hurt so much. He found he could get up again. Maybe because he had to. He went back and looked down. The cop had folded over the railing and gone sliding down it as far as the next turn, the way a kid does on a banister. Only sidewise, on his stomach. Then he dropped off onto the landing, rolled over and lay still, looking up at Paine without seeing him.

Four.

Paine went on up to the roof, but not fast, not easily any more. The steps were like an escalator going the other way, trying to carry him down with them. He went across to the roof of the next flat, and down through that, and came out on the street behind his own. The two buildings were twins, set back to back. The prowl car was already screeching to a stop, out of sight back there at his own doorway. He could hear it over the roofs, on this side.

He was wet across the hip. Then he was wet as far down as the knee. And he hadn't been hit in those places, so he must be bleeding a lot. He saw a taxi and he waved to it, and it backed up and got him. It hurt getting in. He couldn't answer for a minute when the driver asked him where to. His sock felt sticky under his shoe now, from the blood. He wished he could stop it until eight-twenty. He had to meet Pauline on the train, and that was a long time to stay alive.

The driver had taken him off the street and around the corner without waiting for him to be more explicit. He asked where to, a second time.

Paine said, "What time is it?"

"Quarter to six, cap."

Life was awfully short—and awfully sweet. He said, "Take me to the park and drive me around in it." That was the safest thing to do, that was the only place they wouldn't look for you.

He thought, "I've always wanted to drive around in the park. Not go anywhere, just drive around in it slow. I never had the money to do it before."

He had it now. More money than he had time left to
spend it.

The bullet must still be in him. His back didn't hurt, so
it hadn't come out. Something must have stopped it. The
bleeding had let up. He could feel it drying on him. The
pain kept trying to pull him over double though.

The driver noticed it, said: "Are you hurt?"

"No, I've got kind of a cramp, that's all."

"Want me to take you to a drug store?"

Paine smiled weakly. "No, I guess I'll let it ride."

Sundown in the park. So peaceful, so prosaic. Long
shadows across the winding paths. A belated nursemaid
or two pushing a perambulator homeward. A loiterer or
two lingering on the benches in the dusk. A little lake,
with a rowboat on it—a sailor on shore leave rowing his
sweetheart around. A lemonade and popcorn man trun-
dling his wagon home for the day.

Stars were coming out. At times the trees were outlined
black against the copper western sky. At times the whole
thing blurred and he felt as if he were being carried around
in a maelstrom. Each time he fought through and cleared
his senses again. He had to make that train.

"Let me know when it gets to be eight o'clock."

"Sure, cap. It's only quarter to seven now."

A groan was torn from Paine as they hit a lumpy spot
in the driveway. He tried to keep it low, but the driver
must have heard it.

"Still hurts you, huh?" he inquired sympathetically.
"You oughta get it fixed up." He began to talk about his
own indigestion. "Take me, for instance. I'm okay until I
eat tamales and root beer. Any time that I eat tamales
and root beer—"

He shut up abruptly. He was staring fixedly into the
rear-sight mirror. Paine warily clutched his lapels together over his darkened shirt front. He knew it was too
late to do any good.

The driver didn't say anything for a long time. He was thinking it over, and he was a slow thinker. Then finally he suggested off-handedly, "Care to listen to the radio?"

Paine knew what he was out for. He thought, "He wants to see if he can get anything on me over it."

"May as well," the driver urged. "It's thrown in with the fare, won't cost you nothing extra."

"Go ahead," Paine consented. He wanted to see if he could hear anything himself.

It made the pain a little easier to bear, like music always does. "I used to dance, too," Paine thought, listening to the tune, "before I started killing people."

It didn't come over for a long time.

"A city-wide alarm is out for Richard Paine. Paine, who was about to be dispossessed from his flat, shot and killed a finance company employee. Then when Officer Harold Carey answered the alarm, he met the same fate. However, before giving up his life in the performance of his duty, the patrolman succeeded in seriously wounding the desperado. A trail of blood left by the fugitive on the stairs leading up to the roof over which he made good his escape seems to confirm this. He's still at large but probably won't be for long. Watch out for this man, he's dangerous."

"Not if you leave him alone, let him get to that train," Paine thought ruefully. He eyed the suddenly rigid silhouette in front of him. "I'll have to do something about him—now—I guess."

It had come through at a bad time for the driver. Some of the main driveways through the park were heavily trafficked and pretty well lighted. He could have got help from another car. But it happened to come through while they were on a dark, lonely byway with not another machine in sight. Around the next turn the bypass rejoined one of the heavy-traffic arteries. You could hear the hum of traffic from where they were.

"Pull over here," Paine ordered. He'd had the gun out. He was only going to clip him with it, stun him and tie him up until after eight-twenty.

You could tell by the way the driver pulled his breath in short that he'd been wise to Paine ever since the news flash, had only been waiting until they got near one of the exits or got a red light. He braked. Then suddenly he bolted out, tried to duck into the underbrush.

Paine had to get him and get him fast, or he'd get word to the park division. They'd cork up the entrances on him. He knew he couldn't get out and go after him. He pointed low, tried to hit him in the foot or leg, just bring him down.

The driver had tripped over something, gone flat, a moment ahead of the trigger fall. The bullet must have ploughed into his back instead. He was inert when Paine got out to him, but still alive. Eyes open, as though his nerve centers had been paralyzed.

He could hardly stand up himself, but he managed to drag him over to the cab and somehow got him in. He took the cap and put it on his own head.

He could drive—or at least he'd been able to before he was dying. He got under the wheel and took the machine slowly on its way. The sound of the shot must have been lost out in the open, or else mistaken for a backfire; the stream of traffic was rolling obliviously by when he slipped into it unnoticed. He left it again at the earliest opportunity, turned off at the next dark, empty lane that offered itself.

He stopped once more, made his way to the back door, to see how the cabman was. He wanted to help him in some way if he could. Maybe leave him in front of a hospital.

It was too late. The driver's eyes were closed. He was already dead by this time.

Five.

It didn't have any meaning any more. After all, to the

dying death is nothing. "I'll see you again in an hour or so," he said.

He got the driver's coat off him and shrouded him with it, to keep the pale gleam of his face from peering up through the gloom of the cab's interior, in case anyone got too close to the window. He was unequal to the task of getting him out again and leaving him behind in the park. The lights of some passing car might have picked him up too soon. And it seemed more fitting to let him rest in his own cab, anyway.

It was ten to eight now. He'd better start for the station. He might be held up by lights on the way, and the train only stopped a few minutes at the uptown station.

He had to rejoin the main stream of traffic to get out of the park. He hugged the outside of the driveway and trundled along. He went off the road several times. Not because he couldn't drive, but because his senses fogged. He pulled himself and the cab out of it each time. "Train, eight-twenty," he waved before his mind like a red lantern. But like a spend-thrift he was using up years of his life in minutes, and pretty soon he was going to run short.

Once an alarm car passed him, shrieking by, taking a short cut through the park from one side of the city to the other. He wondered if they were after him. He didn't wonder very hard. Nothing mattered much any more. Only eight-twenty—train—

He kept folding up slowly over the wheel and each time it touched his chest, the machine would swerve crazily as though it felt the pain, too. Twice, three times, his fenders were grazed, and he heard faint voices swearing at him from another world, the world he was leaving behind. He wondered if they'd call him names like that if they knew he was dying.

Another thing: he couldn't maintain a steady flow of pressure on the accelerator. The pressure would die out each time, as when current is failing, and the machine would begin drifting to a stop. This happened just as he was leaving the park, crossing the big circular exit plaza. It was controlled by lights and he stalled on a green out in the middle. There was a cop in control on a platform. The cop shot the whistle out of his own mouth blowing it so hard at him. He nearly flung himself off the platform waving him on.

Paine just sat there, helpless.

The cop was coming over to him, raging like a lion. Paine wasn't afraid because of what the back of his cab held; he was long past that kind of fear. But if this cop did anything to keep him from that eight-twenty train—

He reached down finally, gripped his own leg by the ankle, lifted it an inch or two clear of the floor, let it fall back again, and the cab started. It was ludicrous. But then some of the aspects of death often are.

The cop let him go, only because to have detained him longer would have created a worse traffic snarl than there was already.

He was nearly there now. Just a straight run cross-town, then a short one north. It was good he remembered this, because he couldn't see the street signs any more. Sometimes the buildings seemed to lean over above him as though they were about to topple down on him. Sometimes he seemed to be climbing a steep hill, where he knew there wasn't any. But he knew that was just because he was swaying around in the driver's seat.

The same thing happened again a few blocks farther on, directly in front of a large, swank apartment house, just as the doorman came flying out blowing a whistle. He'd caught hold of Paine's rear door and swung it wide before the latter could stop him, even though the cab was still rolling. Two women in evening dress came hurrying out of the entrance behind him, one in advance of the other.

"No—taken," Paine kept trying to say. He was too weak to make his voice heard, or else they ignored it.

And he couldn't push his foot down for a moment.

The foremost one shrieked, "Hurry, Mother. Donald'll never forgive me. I promised him seven-thirty—"

She got one foot on the cab doorstep. Then she just stood there transfixed. She must have seen what was inside; it was better lighted here than in the park.

Paine tore the cab away from her, open door and all, left her standing there petrified, out in the middle of the street in her long white satin gown, staring after him. She was too stunned even to scream.

And then he got there at last. He got a momentary respite, too. Things cleared a little. Like the lights going up in a theater when the show is over, before the house darkens for the night.

The uptown station was built in under a viaduct that carried the overhead tracks across the city streets. He couldn't stop in front of it; no parking was allowed. And there were long lines of cabs on both sides of the no-parking zone. He turned the corner into the little dead-end alley that separated the viaduct from the adjoining buildings. There was a side entrance to the station looking out on it.

Four minutes. It was due in another four minutes. It had already left downtown, was on its way, hurtling somewhere between the two points. He thought, "I better get started. I may have a hard time making it." He wondered if he could stand up at all.

He just wanted to stay where he was and let eternity wash over him.

Two minutes. It was coming in overhead, he could hear it rumbling and ticking along the steel viaduct, then sighing to a long-drawn-out stop.

That sidewalk looked awfully wide, from the cab door to the station entrance. He brought up the last dregs of vitality in him, broke away from the cab, started out, zigzagging and going down lower at the knees every minute. The station door helped pull him up straight again.

He got into the waiting room, and it was so big he knew he'd never be able to cross it. One minute left. So near and yet so far.

The starter was calling it already. "Montreal express— eight-twenty!—Pittsfield, Burlington, Rouse's Point, Montreyall! Bo-o-ard!"

There were rows of lengthwise benches at hand and they helped him bridge the otherwise insuperable length of the waiting room. He dropped into the outside seat in the first row, pulled himself together a little, scrambled five seats over, toppled into that; repeated the process until he was within reach of the ticket barrier. But time was going, the train was going, life was going fast.

Forty-five seconds left. The last dilatory passengers had already gone up. There were two ways of getting up, a long flight of stairs and an escalator.

He wavered toward the escalator, made it. He wouldn't have been able to get by the ticket taker but for his hackman's cap—an eventuality he and Pauline hadn't foreseen.

"Just meeting a party," he mumbled almost unintelligibly, and the slow treadmill started to carry him up.

A whistle blew upstairs on the track platform. Axles and wheel-bases gave a preliminary creak of motion.

It was all he could do to keep his feet even on the escalator. There wasn't anyone in back of him, and if he once went over he was going to go plunging all the way down to the bottom of the long chute. He dug his nails into the ascending hand-belts at both sides, hung on like grim life.

There was a hubbub starting up outside on the street somewhere. He could hear a cop's whistle blowing frenziedly.

A voice shouted: "Which way'd he go?"

Another answered: "I seen him go in the station."

They'd at last found what was in the cab.

A moment after the descending waiting-room ceiling

had cut off his view, he heard a spate of running feet come surging in down there from all directions. But he had no time to think of that now. He was out on the open platform upstairs at last. Cars were skimming silkily by. A vestibule door was coming, with a conductor just lifting himself into it. Paine went toward it, body low, one arm straight out like in a fascist salute.

He gave a wordless cry. The conductor turned, saw him. There was a tug, and he was suddenly sprawled inside on the vestibule floor. The conductor gave him a scathing look, pulled the folding steps in after him, slammed the door.

Too late, a cop, a couple of redcaps, a couple of taxi drivers, came spilling out of the escalator shed. He could hear them yelling a car-length back. The trainmen back there wouldn't open the doors. Suddenly the long, lighted platform snuffed out and the station was gone.

They probably didn't think they'd lost him, but they had. Sure, they'd phone ahead, they'd stop the train to have him taken off at Harmon, where it changed from electricity to coal power. But they wouldn't get him. He wouldn't be on it. Just his body.

Each man knows when he's going to die; he knew he wouldn't even live for five minutes.

He went staggering down a long, brightly lighted aisle. He could hardly see their faces any more. But she'd know him; it'd be all right. The aisle ended, and he had to cross another vestibule. He fell down on his knees, for lack of seat backs to support himself by.

He squirmed up again somehow, got into the next car. Another long, lighted aisle, miles of it.

He was nearly at the end, he could see another vestibule coming. Or maybe that was the door to eternity. Suddenly, from the last seat of all, a hand darted out and claimed him, and there was Pauline's face looking anxiously up at him. He twisted like a wrung-out dishcloth and dropped into the empty outside seat beside her.

"You were going to pass right by," she whispered.

"I couldn't see you clearly, the lights are flickering so."

She looked up at them in surprise, as though for her they were steady.

"I kept my word," he breathed. "I made the train. But oh, I'm tired—and now I'm going to sleep." He started to slip over sidewise toward her. His head dropped onto her lap.

She had been holding her handbag on it, and his fall displaced it. It dropped to the floor, opened, and everything in it spilled out around her feet.

His glazing eyes opened for one last time and centered feebly on the little packet of bills, with a rubber band around them, that had rolled out with everything else.

"Pauline, all that money—where'd you get that much? I only gave you enough to buy the train tickets—"

"Burroughs gave it to me. It's the two hundred and fifty we were talking about for so long. I knew in the end you'd never go near him and ask for it, so I went to him myself—last night right after you left the house. He handed it over willingly, without a word. I tried to tell you that this morning, but you wouldn't let me mention his name. . . ."

12   TA-51